Alfred R. Wallace

A Defence of Modern Spiritualism

Volume 1

Alfred R. Wallace

A Defence of Modern Spiritualism
Volume 1

ISBN/EAN: 9783337340056

Printed in Europe, USA, Canada, Australia, Japan

Cover: Foto ©Andreas Hilbeck / pixelio.de

More available books at **www.hansebooks.com**

A DEFENCE

OF

MODERN SPIRITUALISM.

ALFRED R. WALLACE, F. R. S.,

AUTHOR OF "THE NATURAL HISTORY OF THE MALAY ARCHIPELAGO,"
"EXPLORATIONS ON THE AMAZON," "THE THEORY
OF NATURAL SELECTION,"
ETC., ETC.

WITH A PREFACE

BY EPES SARGENT.

FOURTH THOUSAND.

BOSTON:

COLBY AND RICH,

9 MONTGOMERY PLACE.

1874.

PREFACE.

THE signs are, that both the moral and the religious systems of the future will be greatly modified by the advance of science. They will be more and more conformed to the facts of nature; not only to the facts which a diligent Materialism, working in a single direction, has brought to light, but to the transcendent facts which Modern Spiritualism has restored and proved. The one order of facts is incomplete without the other; and Materialism is as surely doomed to be encircled and transfigured by the wider horizon of Spiritualism, as the Ptolemaic system of the universe was doomed to be superseded by the Copernican.

Unpopular facts often encounter an opposition quite as persistent as that which follows unpopular theories; and so intelligent Spiritualists are not disturbed by the antagonism which their facts have met with from the Huxleys, Tyndalls, Carpenters, and Büchners of our day. All these men, working as they are for science in their different ways, though under the disadvantage of an ignorance of certain phenomena of vast significance, are welcomed as fellow-laborers in the cause of truth by Spiritualists; for the latter, relying on their facts, are confident that genuine Science includes them all, and that every new discovery must be in harmony with all that they hold as true. Opposition to the phenomena, proceeding as it does from lack of knowledge, simply indicates the magnitude and astonishing character of the facts themselves, which could excite such incredulity in the face of such overwhelming testimony.

Among the men of science who have either admitted the facts, or both the facts and the theory, of Spiritualism, are Hare, chemist; Varley, F. R. S., electrician; Flammarion, astronomer; Crookes, F. R. S., chemist; Hoefle, author of the "History of Chemistry;" Nichols, chemist; Fichte, phi-

losopher ; Liais, astronomer ; Hermann Goldschmidt, astronomer, and the discoverer of fourteen planets ; Von Esenbach,
the greatest modern German botanist ; Huggins, F. R. S.,
astronomer and spectroscopist ; De Morgan, mathematician ;
Dille, physicist ; Elliotson, Ashburner, and Gray, physicians
and surgeons. To no one eminent man of science, however, has Spiritualism been more indebted than to Alfred
Russell Wallace, F. R. S., distinguished for his researches
in natural history, paleontology, and anthropology. His
" Defence of Spiritualism," here presented, appeared origi-
nally in the London Fortnightly Review for May and June,
1874. Containing as it does the latest facts, no better tract
for Spiritualists to offer as an answer to their opponents has
yet appeared.

Mr. Wallace, though he arrived, simultaneously with
Mr. Darwin, at similar conclusions in regard to the origin
of species, differs from him on a most important point ; for
Mr. Wallace believes that "a superior intelligence is necessary to account for man." His acquaintance with the phenomena of Spiritualism must always give him, in the sweep
and comprehensiveness of his anthropology, a great advan-
tage over Mr. Darwin. Besides his great work on the
" Natural History of the Malay Archipelago," and an account
of his "Explorations on the Amazon," Mr. Wallace is the
author of " The Theory of Natural Selection," and of many
valuable papers in scientific journals. Dr. Hooker, presi-
dent of the British Scientific Association, wrote, in 1868,
" Of Mr. Wallace, and his many contributions to philosophical biology, it is not easy to speak without enthusiasm ;
for, putting aside their great merits, he, throughout his many
writings, with a modesty as rare as I believe it to be in him
unconscious, forgets his own unquestionable claims to the
honor of having originated, independently of Mr. Darwin,
the theories which he so ably defends."

The testimony of such an investigator as Mr. Wallace
in behalf of the stupendous phenomena of Spiritualism is
not to be lightly put aside or ignored. What can be said in
reply to such an array of facts as he presents ?   E. S.

A DEFENCE

OF

MODERN SPIRITUALISM.

~~~~~~~~~~

IT is with great diffidence, but under an imperative sense of duty, that the present writer accepts the opportunity afforded him of submitting to his readers some general account of a widespread movement, which, though for the most part treated with ridicule or contempt, he believes to embody truths of the most vital importance to human progress.* The subject to be treated is of such vast extent, the evidence concerning it is so varied and so extraordinary, the prejudices that surround it are so inveterate, that it is not possible to do it justice without entering into considerable detail. The reader who ventures on the perusal of the succeeding pages may, therefore, have his patience tried; but if he is able to throw aside his preconceived ideas of what is possible and what is impossible, and in the acceptance or

---

* The following are the more important works which have been used in the preparation of this article: Judge Edmonds's "Spiritual Tracts," New York, 1858–1860. Robert Dale Owen's "Footfalls on the Boundary of Another World," Trübner & Co., 1861. E. Hardinge's "Modern American Spiritualism," New York, 1870. Robert Dale Owen's "Debatable Land between this World and the Next," Trübner & Co., 1871. "Report on Spiritualism of the Committee of the London Dialectical Society," Longmans & Co., 1871. "Year-Book of Spiritualism," Boston and London, 1871. Hudson Tuttle's "Arcana of Spiritualism," Boston, 1871. The Spiritual Magazine, 1861–1874. The Spiritualist Newspaper, 1872–1874. The Medium and Daybreak, 1869–1874.

rejection of the evidence submitted to him will carefully weigh and be solely guided by the nature of the concurrent testimony, the writer ventures to believe that he will not find his time and patience ill bestowed.

Few men, in this busy age, have leisure to read massive volumes devoted to special subjects. They gain much of their general knowledge, outside the limits of their profession or of any peculiar study, by means of periodical literature; and, as a rule, they are supplied with copious and accurate, though general, information. Some of our best thinkers and workers make known the results of their researches to the readers of magazines and reviews; and it is seldom that a writer whose information is meagre, or obtained at second-hand, is permitted to come before the public in their pages as an authoritative teacher. But as regards the subject we are now about to consider, this rule has not hitherto been followed. Those who have devoted many years to an examination of its phenomena have been, in most cases, refused a hearing; while men who have bestowed on it no adequate attention, and are almost wholly ignorant of the researches of others, have alone supplied the information to which a large proportion of the public have had access. In support of this statement it is necessary to refer, with brief comments, to some of the more prominent articles in which the phenomena and pretensions of Spiritualism have been recently discussed.

At the beginning of the present year the readers of this Review were treated to "Experiences of Spiritualism," by a writer of no mean ability, and of thoroughly advanced views. He assures his readers that he "conscientiously endeavored to qualify himself for speaking on this subject" by attending five séances, the details of several of which he narrates; and he comes to the conclusion that mediums are by no means ingenious deceivers, but "jugglers of the most vulgar order;" that the "spiritualistic mind falls a victim to the most patent frauds," and greedily "accepts jugglery as manifestations of spirits"; and, lastly, that the mediums are as credulous as their dupes, and fall straightway into any trap that is laid for them. Now, on the evidence before him, and on the assumption that no more or better evidence would have been forthcoming had he devoted fifty instead of five evenings to the inquiry, the conclusions of Lord Amberley are perfectly logical; but, so far from what he witnessed being a "specimen of the kind of manifestations by which Spiritualists are convinced," a very little acquaintance with the literature of the subject would have shown him that no Spiritualist of any mark was ever convinced by any quantity of such evidence. In an article published since Lord Amberley's—in London Society for February—the author, a barrister and well-known literary man, says:

"It was difficult for me to give in to the idea that solid objects could be conveyed, invisibly, through closed doors, or that heavy furniture could be moved without the interposition of hands. Philosophers will say these things are absolutely impossible; nevertheless, it is absolutely certain that they do occur. I have met in the houses of private friends, as witnesses of these phenomena, persons whose testimony would go for a good deal in a court of justice. They have included peers, members of parliament, diplomatists of the highest rank, judges, barristers, physicians, clergymen, members of learned societies, chemists, engineers, journalists, and thinkers of all sorts and degrees. They have suggested and carried into effect tests of the most rigid and satisfactory character. The media (all non-professional) have been searched before and after séances. The precaution has even been taken of providing them unexpectedly with other apparel. They have been tied; they have been sealed; they have been secured in every cunning and dexterous manner that ingenuity could devise, but no deception has been discovered and no imposture brought to light. Neither was there any motive for imposture. No fee or reward of any kind depended upon the success or non-success of the manifestations."

Now here we have a nice question of probabilities. We must either believe that Lord Amberley is almost infinitely more acute than Mr. Dunphy and his host of eminent friends —so that after five séances (most of them failures) he has got to the bottom of a mystery in which they, notwithstanding their utmost endeavors, still hopelessly flounder—or, that the noble lord's acuteness does not surpass the combined acuteness of all these persons; in which case their much larger experience, and their having witnessed many things Lord Amberley has not witnessed, must be held to have the greater weight, and to show, at all events, that all mediums are not "jugglers of the most vulgar order."

In October last the New Quarterly Magazine, in its opening number, had an article entitled "A Spiritualistic Séance;" but which proved to be an account of certain ingenious contrivances by which some of the phenomena usual at séances were imitated, and both Spiritualists and skeptics deceived and confounded. This appears at first sight to be an exposure of Spiritualism, but it is really very favorable to its pretensions; for it goes on the assumption that the marvelous phenomena witnessed do really occur, but are produced by various mechanical contrivances. In this case the rooms above, below, and at the side of that in which the séance was held had to be prepared with specially constructed machinery, with assistants to work it. The apparatus, as described, would cost at least £100, and would then only serve to produce a few fixed phenomena, such as happen frequently in private houses and at the lodgings of mediums who have not exclusive possession of any of the adjoining rooms, or the means of obtaining expensive machinery and hired assistants. The article bears internal evidence of being altogether a fictitious narrative; but it helps to demonstrate, if any demonstration is required, that the phenomena which occur under such protean forms and varied conditions, and in private houses quite as often as at the apartments of the mediums, are in no way produced by machinery.

Perhaps the most prominent recent attack on Spiritualism was that in the Quarterly Review for October, 1871, which is known to have been written by an eminent physiologist, and did much to blind the public to the real nature of the movement. This article, after giving a light sketch of the reported phenomena, entered into some details as to planchette-writing and table-lifting—facts on which no Spiritualist depends as evidence to a third party—and then proceeded to define its standpoint as follows:

"Our position, then, is that the so-called spiritual communications come from *within*, not from without, the individuals who suppose themselves to be the recipients of them; that they belong to the class termed 'subjective' by physiologists and psychologists, and that the movements by which they are expressed, whether the tilting of tables or the writing of planchettes, are really produced by their own muscular action exerted independently of their own wills and quite unconsciously to themselves."

Several pages are then devoted to accounts of séances which, like Lord Amberley's, were mostly failures; and to the experiences of a Bath clergyman who believed that the communications came from devils; and, generally, such weak and inconclusive phenomena only are adduced as can be easily explained by the well-worn formulæ of "unconscious cerebration," "expectant attention," and "unconscious muscular action." A few of the more startling physical phenomena are mentioned merely to be discredited and the judgment of the witnesses impugned; but no attempt is made to place before the reader any information as to the amount or the weight of the testimony to such phenomena, or to the long series of diverse phenomena which lead up to and confirm them. Some of the experiments of Prof. Hare and Mr. Crookes are quoted and criticised in the spirit of assuming that these experienced physicists were ignorant of the simplest principles of mechanics, and failed to use the most ordinary precautions. Of the numerous and varied cases on record, of heavy bodies being moved without direct or indirect contact by any human being, no notice is taken, except so far as quoting Mr. C. F. Varley's statement, that he had seen, in broad daylight, a small table moved ten feet, with no one near it but himself, and not touched by him—"as an example of the manner in which minds of this limited order are apt to become the dupes of their own imaginings."

This article, like the others here referred to, shows in the writer an utter forgetfulness of the maxim, that an argument is not answered till it is answered at its best. Amid the vast mass of recorded facts now accumulated by Spiritualists, there is, of course, much that is weak and inconclusive, much that is of no value as evidence, except to those who have independent reasons for faith in them. From this undigested mass it is the easiest thing in the world to pick out arguments that can be refuted and facts that can be explained away; but what is that to the purpose? It is not these that have convinced any one ; but those weightier, oft-repeated and oft-tested facts which the writers referred to invariably ignore.

Prof. Tyndall has also given the world (in his "Fragments of Science," published in 1871) some account of his attempt to investigate these phenomena. Again, we have a minute record of a séance which was a failure, and in which the Professor, like Lord Amberley, easily imposed on some too credulous Spiritualists by improvising a few manifestations of his own. The article in question is dated as far back as 1864. We may therefore conclude that the Professor has not seen much of the subject ; nor can he have made himself acquainted with what others have seen and carefully verified, or he would hardly have thought his communication worthy of the place it occupies among original researches and positive additions to human knowledge. Both its facts and its reasonings have been well replied to by Mr. Patrick Fraser Alexander, in his little work entitled "Spiritualism ; a Narrative and a Discussion," which we recommend to those who care to see how a very acute yet unprejudiced mind looks at the phenomena, and how inconclusive, even from a scientific standpoint, are the experiences adduced by Prof. Tyndall.

The discussion in the Pall Mall Gazette in 1868, and a considerable private correspondence, indicates that scientific men almost invariably assume that, in this inquiry, they should be permitted, at the very outset, to impose conditions; and if, under such conditions, nothing happens, they consider it a proof of imposture or delusion. But they well know that, in all other branches of research, Nature, not they, determines the essential conditions, without a compliance with which no experiment will succeed. These conditions have to be learnt by a patient questioning of Nature, and they are different for each branch of science. How much more may they be expected to differ in an inquiry which deals with subtle forces of the nature of which the physicist is wholly and absolutely ignorant! To ask to be allowed to deal with these unknown phenomena as he has hitherto dealt with known phenomena, is practically to prejudge the question, since it assumes that both are governed by the same laws.

From the sketch which has now been given of the recent treatment of the subject by popular and scientific writers, we can summarize pretty accurately their mental attitude in regard to it. They have seen very little of the phenomena themselves, and they cannot believe that others have seen much more. They have encountered people who are easily deceived by a little unexpected trickery, and they conclude that the convictions of Spiritualists generally are founded on phenomena produced, either consciously or unconsciously, in a similar way. They are so firmly convinced, on *á priori* grounds, that the more remarkable phenomena said to happen do not really happen, that they will back their conviction against the direct testimony of any body of men, preferring to believe that they are all the victims of some mysterious delusion whenever imposture is out of the question. To influence persons in this frame of mind, it is evident that *more* personal testimony to isolated facts is utterly useless. They have, to use the admirable expression of Dr. Carpenter, "no place in the existing fabric of their thought into which such facts can be fitted." It is necessary, therefore, to modify the "fabric of thought" itself; and it appears to the present writer that this can best be done by a general historic sketch of the subject, and by showing, by separate lines of inquiry, how wide and varied is the evidence, and how remarkably these lines converge toward one uniform conclusion. The endeavor will be made to indicate, by typical examples of each class of evidence and without unnecessary detail, the cumulative force of the argument.

HISTORICAL SKETCH.

Modern Spiritualism dates from March, 1848; it being then that, for the first time, intelligent communications were held with the unknown cause of the mysterious knockings and other sounds, similar to those which had disturbed the Mompesson and Wesley families in the seventeenth and eighteenth centuries. This discovery was made by Miss Kate Fox, a girl of nine years old, and the first recognized example of an extensive class now known as mediums. It is worthy of remark that this very first "modern spiritual manifestation" was subjected to the test of unlimited examination by all the inhabitants of the village of Hydesville, New York. Though all were utter skeptics, no one could discover any cause for the noises, which continued, though with less violence, when all the children had left the house. Nothing is more common than the remark that it is absurd and illogical to impute noises, of which we cannot discover the cause, to the agency of spirits. So it undoubtedly is when the noises are merely noises; but is it so illogical when these noises turn out to be signals, and signals which spell out a fact, which·fact, though wholly unknown to all present, turns out to be true? Yet, on this very first occasion, twenty-six years ago, the signals declared that a murdered man was buried in the cellar of the house; it indicated the exact spot in the cellar under which the body lay; and upon digging there, at a depth of six or seven feet, considerable portions of a human skeleton were found. Yet more: the name of the murdered man was given, and it was ascertained that such a person had visited that very house and had disappeared five years before, and had never been heard of since. The signals further declared that he, the murdered man, was the signaller; and as all the witnesses had satisfied themselves that the signals were not made by any living person or by any assignable cause, the logical conclusion from the facts was, that it *was* the spirit* of the murdered man; although such a conclusion

---

* It may be as well here to explain that the word "spirit," which is often considered to be so objectionable by scientific men, is used throughout this article (or at all events in the earlier portions of it) merely to avoid circumlocution, in the sense of the " intelligent cause of the phenomena," and not as implying "the spirits of the dead," unless so expressly stated.

might be to some in the highest degree improbable, and to others in the highest degree absurd.

The Misses Fox now became involuntary mediums, and the family (which had removed to the city of Rochester) were accused of imposture, and offered to submit the children to examination by a committee of townsmen appointed in public meeting. Three committees were successively appointed; the last, composed of violent skeptics who had accused the previous committees of stupidity or connivance. But all three, after unlimited investigation, were forced to declare that the cause of the phenomena was undiscoverable. The sounds occurred on the wall and floor while the mediums, after being thoroughly searched by ladies, "stood on pillows, barefooted, and with their clothes tied round their ankles." The last and most skeptical committee reported that, "They had heard sounds, and failed utterly to discover their origin. They had proved that neither machinery nor imposture had been used; and their questions, *many of them being mental*, were answered correctly." When we consider that the mediums were two children under twelve years of age, and the examiners utterly skeptical American citizens, thoroughly resolved to detect imposture, and urged on by excited public meetings, it may perhaps be considered that even at this early stage the question of imposture or delusion was pretty well settled in the negative.

In a short time persons who sat with the Misses Fox found themselves to have similar powers in a greater or less degree; and in two or three years the movement had spread over a large part of the United States, developing into a variety of strange forms, encountering the most violent skepticism and the most rancorous hostility, yet always progressing, and making converts even among the most enlightened and best educated classes. In 1851, some of the most intelligent men in New York—judges, senators, doctors, lawyers, merchants, clergymen and authors—formed themselves into a society for investigation. Judge Edmonds was one of these; and a sketch of the kind and amount of evidence that was required to convince him will be given further on. In 1854 a second spiritual society was formed in New York. It had the names of four judges and two physicians among its Vice-Presidents, showing that the movement had by this time become respectable, and that men in high social positions were not afraid of identifying themselves with it. A little later Professor Mapes, an eminent agricultural chemist, was led to undertake the investigation of Spiritualism. He formed a circle of twelve friends, most of them men of talent, and skeptics, who bound themselves to sit together weekly, with a medium, twenty times. For the first eighteen evenings the phenomena were so trivial and unsatisfactory that most of the party felt disgusted at the loss of time; but the last two sittings produced phenomena of so startling a character that the investigation was continued by the same circle *for four years, and all became Spiritualists.*

By this time the movement had spread into every part of the Union, and, notwithstanding that its adherents were abused as impostors or dupes, that they were in several cases expelled from colleges and churches and were confined as lunatics, and that the whole thing was "explained" over and over again—it has continued to spread up to the present hour. The secret of this appears to have been, that the explanations given never applied to the phenomena continually occurring, and of which there were numerous witnesses. A medium was raised in the air in a crowded room in full daylight. ("Modern American Spiritualism," p. 279.) A scientific skeptic prepared a small portable apparatus, by which he could produce an instantaneous illumination; and, taking it to a dark séance at which numerous musical instruments were played, suddenly lighted up the room while a large drum was being violently beaten, in the certain expectation of revealing the impostor to the whole company. But what they all saw was the drumstick itself beating the drum, with no human being near it. It struck a few more blows, then rose into the air and descended gently on to the shoulder of a lady. (Same work, p. 337.) At Toronto, Canada, in a well-lighted room, an accompaniment to a song was played on a closed and locked piano. (Same work, p. 463.) Communications were given in raised letters on the arm of an ignorant servant girl, who often could not read them. They sometimes appeared while she was at her household work, and after being read by her master or mistress would disappear. (Same work, p. 196.) Letters closed in any number of envelopes, sealed up or even pasted together over the whole of the written surface, were read and answered by certain mediums in whom this special power was developed. It mattered not what language the letters were written in; and it is upon record that letters in German, Greek, Hebrew, Arabic, Chinese, French, Welsh and Mexican, have been correctly answered in the corresponding languages by a medium who knew none of them. (Judge Edmonds's "Letters on Spiritualism," pp. 59-103, Appendix.) Other mediums drew portraits of deceased persons whom they had never known or heard of. Others healed diseases. But those who helped most to spread the belief were, perhaps, the trance speakers, who, in eloquent and powerful language, developed the principles and the uses of Spiritualism, answered objections, spread abroad a knowledge of the phenomena, and thus induced skeptics to inquire into the facts ; and inquiry was almost invariably followed by conversion. Having repeatedly listened to three of these speakers who have visited this country, I can bear witness that they fully equal, and not unfrequently surpass our best orators and preachers ; whether in finished eloquence, in close and logical argument, or in the readiness with which appropriate and convincing replies are made to all objectors. They are also remarkable for the perfect courtesy and suavity of their manner, and for the extreme patience and gentleness with which they meet the most violent opposition and the most unjust accusations.

Men of the highest rank and greatest ability became convinced by these varied phenomena. No amount of education, of legal, medical or scientific training, was proof against the overwhelming force of the facts, whenever these facts were systematically and perseveringly inquired into. The number of Spiritualists in the Union is, according to those who have the best means of judging, from eight to eleven millions. This is the estimate of Judge Edmonds, who has had extensive correspondence on the subject with every part of the United States. The Hon. R. D. Owen, who has also had great opportunities of knowing the facts, considers it to be approximately correct ; and it is affirmed by the editors of the "Year-Book of Spiritualism" for 1871. These numbers have been held to be absurdly exaggerated by persons having less information, especially by strangers who have made superficial inquiries in America ; but it must be remembered that the Spiritualists are to a very limited extent an organized body, and that the mass of them make no public profession of their belief, but still remain members of some denominational church—circumstances that would greatly deceive an outsider. Nevertheless, the organization is of considerable extent. There were in America, in 1870, 20 State Associations and 105 Societies of Spiritualists, 207 lecturers, and about the same number of public mediums.

In other parts of the world the movement has progressed

more or less rapidly. Several of the more celebrated American mediums have visited this country, and not only made converts in all classes of society, but led to the formation of private circles and the discovery of mediumistic power in hundreds of families. There is scarcely a city or a considerable town in Continental Europe at the present moment where Spiritualists are not reckoned by hundreds, if not by thousands. There are said, on good authority, to be fifty thousand avowed Spiritualists in Paris and ten thousand in Lyons; and the numbers in England may be roughly estimated by the fact that there are four exclusively spiritual periodicals, one of which has a circulation of five thousand weekly.

DEDUCTIONS FROM THE PRECEDING SKETCH.

Before proceeding to a statement of the evidence which has convinced the more educated and more skeptical converts, let us consider briefly the bearing of the undoubted fact, that (to keep within bounds) many thousands of well-informed men, belonging to all classes of society and all professions, have, in each of the great civilized nations of the world, acknowledged the objective reality of these phenomena; although, almost without exception, they at first viewed them with dislike or contempt, as impostures or delusions. There is nothing parallel to it in the history of human thought; because there never before existed so strong and apparently so well-founded a conviction that phenomena of this kind never have happened and never can happen. It is often said, that the number of adherents to a belief is no proof of its truth. This remark justly applies to most religions whose arguments appeal to the emotions and the intellect but not to the evidence of the senses. It is equally just as applied to a great part of modern science. The almost universal belief in gravitation, and in the undulatory theory of light, does not render them in any degree more probable; because very few indeed of the believers have tested the facts which most convincingly demonstrate those theories, or are able to follow out the reasoning by which they are demonstrated. It is for the most part a blind belief accepted upon authority. But with these spiritual phenomena the case is very different. They are to most men so new, so strange, so incredible, so opposed to their whole habit of thought, so apparently opposed to the pervading scientific spirit of the age, that they cannot and do not accept them on second-hand evidence, as they do almost every other kind of knowledge. The thousands or millions of Spiritualists, therefore, represent to a very large extent men who have witnessed, examined, and tested the evidence for themselves, over and over and over again, till that which they had at first been unable to admit *could* be true, they have at last been compelled to acknowledge *is* true. This accounts for the utter failure of all the attempted "exposures" and "explanations" to convince one solitary believer of his error. The exposers and explainers have never got beyond those first difficulties which constitute the *pons asinorum* of Spiritualism, which every believer has to get over, but at which early stage of investigation no converts are ever made. By explaining table-turning, or table-tilting, or raps, you do not influence a man who was never convinced by these, but who, in broad daylight, sees objects move without contact, and behave as if guided by intelligent beings; and who sees this in a variety of forms, in a variety of places, and under such varied and stringent conditions, as to make the fact to him just as real as the movement of iron to the magnet. By explaining automatic writing (which itself convinces no one but the writer, and not always even him), you do not affect the belief of the man who has obtained writing when neither pencil nor paper was touched by any one ; or has seen a hand not attached to any human body take up a pencil and write ; or, as Mr. Andrew Leighton, of Liverpool, testifies, has seen a pencil rise of itself on a table and write the words : "*And is this world of strife to end in dust at last ?*" Thus it is that there are so few recantations or perverts in Spiritualism ; so few, that it may be truly said there are none. After much inquiry and reading I can find no example of a man who, having acquired a good personal knowledge of all the chief phases of the phenomena, has subsequently come to disbelieve in their reality. If the "explanations" and "exposures" were good for anything, or if it were an imposture to expose or a delusion to explain, this could not be the case, because there are numbers of men who have become convinced of the facts, but who have not accepted the spiritual theory. These are, for the most part, in an uncomfortable and unsettled frame of mind, and would gladly welcome an explanation which really explained anything— but they find it not. As an eminent example of this class, I may mention Dr. J. Lockhart Robertson, long one of the editors of the Journal of Mental Science—a physician who, having made mental disease his special study, would not be easily taken in by any psychological delusions. The phenomena he witnessed fourteen years ago were of a violent character; a very strong table being, at his own request and in his own house, broken to pieces while he held the medium's hands. He afterwards himself tried to break a remaining leg of the table, but failed to do so after exerting all his strength. Another table was tilted over while all the party sat on it. He subsequently had a sitting with Mr. Home, and witnessed the usual phenomena occurring with that extraordinary medium —such as the accordion playing "most wonderful music without any human agency," "a shadow hand, not that of any one present, which lifts a pencil and writes with it," &c., &c.; and he says that he can "no more doubt the physical manifestations of (so-called) Spiritualism than he would any other fact—as, for example, the fall of an apple to the ground of which his senses informed him." His record of these phenomena, with the confirmation by a friend who was present, is published in the "Dialectical Society's Report on Spiritualism," p. 247; and, at a meeting of Spiritualists in 1870, he reasserted the facts, but denied their spiritual origin. To such a man the Quarterly Reviewer's explanations are worthless; yet it may be safely said, that every advanced Spiritualist has seen more remarkable, more varied, and even more inexplicable phenomena than those recorded by Dr. Robertson, and is therefore still further out of reach of the arguments referred to, which are indeed only calculated to convince those who know little or nothing of the matter.

EVIDENCE OF THE FACTS.

The subject of the evidences of the objective phenomena of Spiritualism is such a large one that it will be only possible here to give a few typical examples, calculated to show how wide is their range, and how conclusively they reach every objection that the most skeptical have brought against them. This may perhaps be best done by giving, in the first place, an outline of the career of two or three well-known mediums; and, in the second, a sketch of the experiences and investigations of a few of the more remarkable converts to Spiritualism.

Career of Remarkable Mediums.—Miss Kate Fox, the little girl of nine years old, who, as already stated, was the first
2

"medium" in the modern sense of the term, has continued to possess the same power for twenty-six years. At the very earliest stages of the movement, skeptic after skeptic, committee after committee endeavored to discover "the trick;" but if it was a trick this little girl baffled them all, and the proverbial acuteness of the Yankee was of no avail. In 1860, when Dr. Robert Chambers visited America, he suggested to his friend, Robert Dale Owen, the use of a balance to test the lifting power. They accordingly, without prearrangement with the medium, took with them a powerful steelyard, and suspended from it a dining-table weighing one hundred and twenty-one pounds. Then, under a bright gas-light, the feet of the two mediums (Miss Fox and her sister) being both touched by the feet of the gentlemen, and the hands of all present being held over but not touching the table, it was made lighter or heavier at request, so as to weigh at one time only sixty, at another one hundred and thirty-four pounds. This experiment, be it remembered, was identical with one proposed by Faraday himself as being conclusive. Mr. Owen had many sittings with Miss Fox, for the purpose of test, and the precautions he took were extraordinary. He sat with her alone; he frequently changed the room without notice; he examined every article of furniture; he locked the doors and fastened them with strips of paper privately sealed; he held both the hands of the medium. Under these conditions various phenomena occurred, the most remarkable being the illumination of a piece of paper (which he had brought himself, cut of a peculiar size, and privately marked,) showing a dark hand writing on the floor. The paper afterwards rose up on to the table with legible writing upon it, containing a promise which was subsequently verified. ("Debatable Land," p. 293.)

But Miss Fox's powers were most remarkably shown in the séances with Mr. Livermore, a well-known New York banker, and an entire skeptic before commencing these experiments. These sittings were more than three hundred in number, extending over five years. They took place in four different houses (Mr. Livermore's and the medium's being both changed during this period), under tests of the most rigid description. The chief phenomenon was the appearance of a tangible, visible and audible figure of Mr. Livermore's deceased wife, sometimes accompanied by a male figure, purporting to be Dr. Franklin. The former figure was often most distinct and absolutely life-like. It moved various objects in the room. It wrote messages on cards. It was sometimes formed out of a luminous cloud, and again vanished before the eyes of the witnesses. It allowed a portion of its dress to be cut off, which, though at first of strong and apparently gauzy material texture, yet in a short time melted away and became invisible. Flowers which melted away were also given. These phenomena occurred best when Mr. L. and the medium were alone; but two witnesses were occasionally admitted, who tested everything and confirmed Mr. L.'s testimony. One of these was Mr. Livermore's physician, the other his brother-in-law; the latter previously a skeptic. The details of these wonderful séances were published in the Spiritual Magazine in 1862 and 1863; and the more remarkable are given in Owen's "Debatable Land," from which work a good idea may be formed of the great variety of the phenomena that occurred and the stringent character of the tests employed.

Miss Fox recently came to England, and here also her powers have been tested by a competent man of science, and found to be all that has been stated. She is now married to an English barrister, and some of the strange phenomena which have so long accompanied her attach themselves to her infant child, even when its mother is away, to the great alarm of the nurse. We have here, therefore, a career of twenty-six years of mediumship of the most varied and remarkable character; mediumship which has been scrutinized and tested from the first hour of its manifestation down to this day, and with one invariable result—that no imposture or attempt at imposture has ever been discovered, and no cause ever been suggested that will account for the phenomena except that advanced by Spiritualists.

Mr. Daniel D. Home is perhaps the best known medium in the world; and his powers have been open to examination for at least twenty years. Nineteen years ago Sir David Brewster and Lord Brougham had a sitting with him—suffi ciently acute and eminent observers, and both, of course thorough skeptics. In the "Home Life of Sir David Brew ster," we have, fortunately, his own record of this sitting made *at the time,* although six months later, in a letter to the Morning Advertiser, he made the contradictory statement: "I saw enough to satisfy myself they could all be produced by human hands and feet." He says: "The table actually rose from the ground when no hand was upon it;" and "a small hand-bell was laid down with its mouth on the carpet, and it actually rang when nothing could have touched it. The bell was then placed on the other side, still upon the carpet, and it came over to me and placed itself in my hand. It did the same to Lord Brougham." And he adds, speaking for both, " We could give no explanation of them, and could not conjecture how they could be produced by any kind of mecnanism." Coming from the author of "Letters on Natural Magic," this is pretty good testimony.

These and far more marvelous phenomena have been repeated from that day to this many thousands of times, and almost always in private houses at which Mr. Home visits. Everybody testifies to the fact that he offers the most ample facilities for investigation ; and to this I can myself bear witness, having been invited by him to examine as closely as I pleased an accordion, held by his one hand, keys downward, and in that position playing very sweetly. But perhaps the best-attested and most extraordinary phenomenon connected with Mr. Home's mediumship is what is called the fire-test. In a state of trance he takes a glowing coal from the hottest part of a bright fire and carries it round the room, so that every one may see and feel that it is a real one. This is testified by Mr. H. D. Jencken, Lord Lindsay, Lord Adare, Miss Douglas, Mr. S. C. Hall, and many others. But, more strange still, when in this state he can detect the same power in other persons, or convey it to them. A lump of red-hot coal was once placed on Mr. S. C. Hall's head in the presence of Lord Lindsay and four other persons. Mrs. Hall, in a communication to the Earl of Dunraven (given in the Spiritual Magazine, 1870, p. 178), says :

"Mr. Hall was seated nearly opposite to where I sat ; and I saw Mr. Home, after standing about half a minute at the back of Mr. Hall's chair, deliberately place the lump of burning coal on his head ! I have often wondered that I was not frightened, but I was not ; I had perfect faith that he would not be injured. Some one said, 'Is it not hot?' Mr. Hall answered, 'Warm, but not hot !' Mr. Home had moved a little way, but returned, still in a trance ; he smiled, and seemed quite pleased, and then proceeded to draw up Mr. Hall's white hair over the red coal. The white hair had the appearance of silver thread over the red coal. Mr. Home drew the hair into a sort of pyramid, the coal, still red, showing beneath the hair."

When taken off the head—which it had not in the slightest degree injured or singed the hair—others attempted to touch it, and were burnt. Lord Lindsay and Miss Douglas have

also had hot coals placed in their hands, and they describe
them as feeling rather cold than hot; though at the same time
they burn any one else, and even scorch the face of the hold-
er if approached too closely. The same witnesses also testify that Mr. Home has placed red-hot coals inside his waist-
coat without scorching his clothes, and has put his face into
the middle of the fire, his hair falling into the flames, yet not
being the least singed. The same power of resisting fire can
be temporarily given to inanimate objects. Mr. H. Nisbet,
of Glasgow, states ("Human Nature," Feb., 1870) that, in
his own house, in January, 1870, Mr. Home placed a red-hot
coal in the hands of a lady and gentleman, which they only
felt warm; and then placed the same piece on a folded newspaper, burning a hole through eight layers of paper. He then
took a fresh and blazing coal and laid it on the same newspaper, carrying it about the room for three minutes, when
the paper was found, this time, not to have been the least
burnt. Lord Lindsay further declares—and as one of the few
noblemen who do real scientific work his evidence must be of
some value—that on eight occasions he has had red-hot coals
placed on his own hand by Home without injury. Mr. W.
H. Harrison ("Spiritualist," March 15th, 1870) saw him take
a large coal, which covered the palm of his hand, and stood
six or seven inches high. As he walked about the room it
threw a ruddy glow on the walls, and when he came to the
table with it, the heat was felt in the faces of all present.
The coal was thus held for five minutes. These phenomena
have now happened scores of times in the presence of scores
of witnesses. They are facts, of the reality of which there
can be no doubt; and they are altogether inexplicable by the
known laws of physiology and heat.

The powers of Mr. Home have lately been independently
tested by Serjeant Cox and Mr. Crookes, and both these gentlemen emphatically proclaim that he invites tests and courts
examination. Serjeant Cox, in his own house, has had a new
accordion (purchased by himself that very day) play by itself, in his own hand, while Mr. Home was playing the piano.
Mr. Home then took the accordion in his left hand, holding it
with the keys downwards while playing the piano with his
right hand, "and it played beautifully in accompaniment to
the piano, for at least a quarter of an hour." ("What Am
I?" Vol. II., p. 388.)

As to the possibility of these things being produced by
trick, if further evidence than their mere statement be re-

quired, we have the following by Mr. T. Adolphus Trollope,
who says, "I may also mention that Bosco, one of the greatest professors of legerdemain ever known, in a conversation
with me upon the subject, utterly scouted the idea of the possibility of such phenomena as I saw produced by Mr. Home
being performed by any of the resources of his art."

Mr. Home's life has been to a great extent a public one.
He has spent much of his time as a guest in the houses of
people of rank and talent. He numbers among his friends
many who are eminent in science, art, and literature—men
certainly not inferior in perceptive or reasoning power to
those who, not having witnessed the phenomena, disbelieve
in their occurrence. For twenty years he has been exposed
to the keen scrutiny and never-ceasing suspicion of innumerable inquirers; yet no proof has ever been given of trickery,
no particle of machinery or apparatus ever been detected.
But the phenomena are so stupendous that, if impostures,
they could only be performed by machinery of the most elaborate, varied and cumbrous nature, requiring the aid of several assistants and confederates. The theory that they are
delusions is equally untenable, unless it is admitted that there
is no possible means of distinguishing delusion from reality.

The last medium to whose career I shall call attention is
Mrs. Guppy (formerly Miss Nichol), and in this case I can
give some personal testimony. I knew Miss Nichol before
she had ever heard of Spiritualism, table-rapping, or anything
of the kind, and we first discovered her powers on asking her
to sit for experiment in my house. This was in November,
1866, and for some months we had constant sittings, and I
was able to watch and test the progress of her development.
I first satisfied myself of the rising of a small table completely off the floor, when three or four persons (including Miss
N.) placed their hands on it. I tested this by secretly attach-
ing threads or thin strips of paper underneath the claws, so
that they must be broken if any one attempted to raise the table with their feet, the only available means of doing so. The
table still rose a full foot off the floor in broad daylight. In
order to show this to friends with less trouble, I made a cylinder of hoops and brown paper, in which I placed the table so
as to keep feet and dresses away from it while it rose, which
it did as freely as before. Perhaps more marvelous was the
placing of Miss N. herself on the table; for although this always happened in the dark, yet, under the conditions to be

named, deception was impossible. I will relate one sitting of which I have notes. We sat in a friend's house, round a centre table, under a glass chandelier. A friend of mine, but a perfect stranger to all the rest, sat next Miss Nichol and held both her hands. Another person had matches ready to strike a light when required. What occurred was as follows : First, Miss Nichol's chair was drawn away from under her, and she was obliged to stand up, my friend still holding both her hands. In a minute or two more I heard a slight sound, such as might be produced by a person placing a wine-glass on the table, and at the same time a very slight rustling of clothes and tinkling of the glass pendants of the chandelier. Immediately my friend said, "She is gone from me." A light was at once struck, and we found Miss N. quietly seated in her chair on the centre of the table, her head just touching the chandelier. My friend declared that Miss N. seemed to glide noiselessly out of his hands. She was very stout and heavy, and to get her chair on the table, to get upon it herself, in the dark, noiselessly, and almost instantaneously, with five or six persons close around her, appeared, and still appears to me, knowing her intimately, to be physically impossible.

Another very curious and beautiful phenomenon was the production of delicate musical sounds, without any object calculated to produce them being in the room. On one occasion a German lady, who was a perfect stranger to Miss Nichol, and had never been at a séance before, was present. She sang several German songs, and most delicate music, like a fairy musical-box, accompanied her throughout. She sang four or five different songs of her own choice, and all were so accompanied. This was in the dark, but hands were joined all the time.

The most remarkable feature of this lady's mediumship is the production of flowers and fruits in closed rooms. The first time this occurred was at my own house at a very early stage of her development. All present were my own friends. Miss Nichol had come early to tea, it being mid-winter, and she had been with us in a very warm gas-lighted room four hours before the flowers appeared. The essential fact is, that upon a bare table in a small room closed and dark (the adjoining room and passage being well lighted), a quantity of flowers appeared, which were not there when we put out the gas a few minutes before. They consisted of anemones, tulips, chrysanthemums, Chinese primroses, and several ferns. All were absolutely fresh, as if just gathered from a conservatory. They were covered with a fine, cold dew. Not a petal was crumpled or broken, not the most delicate point or pinnule of the ferns was out of place. I dried and preserved the whole, and have, attached to them, the attestation of all present that they had no share, as far as they knew, in bringing the flowers into the room. I believed at the time, and still believe, that it was absolutely impossible for Miss N. to have concealed them so long, to have kept them so perfect, and, above all, to produce them covered throughout with a most beautiful coating of dew, just like that which collects on the outside of a tumbler when filled with very cold water on a hot day.

Similar phenomena have occurred hundreds of times since, in many houses and under various conditions. Sometimes the flowers have been in vast quantities, heaped upon the table. Often flowers or fruits asked for are brought. A friend of mine asked for a sunflower, and one six feet high fell upon the table, having a large mass of earth about its roots. One of the most striking tests was at Florence, with Mr. T. Adolphus Trollope, Mrs. Trollope, Miss Blagden, and Colonel Harvey. The room was searched by the gentlemen; Mrs. Guppy was undressed and redressed by Mrs. Trollope, every article of her clothing being examined. Mr. and Mrs. Guppy were both firmly held while at the table. In about ten minutes all the party exclaimed that they smelt flowers, and, on lighting a candle, both Mrs. Guppy's and Mr. Trollope's arms were found covered with jonquils, which filled the room with their odor. Mr. Guppy and Mr. Trollope both relate this in substantially the same terms. (" Dialectical Society's Report on Spiritualism,'' pp. 277 and 372.)

Surely these are phenomena about which there can be no mistake. What theories have ever been proposed by our scientific teachers which even attempt to account for them? Delusion it cannot be, for the flowers are real and can be preserved, and imposture under the conditions described is even less credible. If the gentlemen who came forward to enlighten the public on the subject of " so-called spiritual manifestations " do not know of the various classes of phenomena that have now been indicated, and the weight of the testimony in support of them, they are palpably unqualified for the task they have undertaken. That they do know of them, but keep back their knowledge, while putting forward trivialities easy to laugh at or expose, is a supposition I cannot for a moment entertain. Before leaving this part of the subject, it is well to note the fact of the marked individuality of each medium. They are not copies of each other, but each one develops a characteristic set of phenomena—a fact highly suggestive of some unconscious occult power in the individual, and wholly opposed to the idea of either imposture or delusion, both of which almost invariably copy preëxisting models.

Investigations by some Notable Skeptics.—In giving some account of how a few of the more important converts to Spiritualism became convinced, we are of course limited to those who have given their experiences to the public. I will first take the case of the eminent American lawyer, the Hon. J. W. Edmonds, commonly called Judge Edmonds; and it may be as well to let English skeptics know what he is thought of by his countrymen. When he first became a Spiritualist he was greatly abused; and it was even declared that he consulted the spirits on his judicial decisions. To defend himself, he published an "Appeal to the Public," giving a full account of the inquiries which resulted in his conversion. In noticing this, the New York Evening Mirror said: "John W. Edmonds, the Chief Justice of the Supreme Court of this District, is an able lawyer, an industrious judge and a good citizen. For the last eight years occupying without interruption the highest judicial stations, whatever may be his faults no one can justly accuse him of a lack of ability, industry, honesty or fearlessness. No one can doubt his general saneness, or can believe for a moment that the ordinary operations of his mind are not as rapid, accurate and reliable as ever. Both by the practitioners and suitors at his bar he is recognized as the head, in fact and in merit, of the Supreme Court for this District." A few years later he published a series of letters on Spiritualism in the New York Tribune; and in the first of these he gives a compact summary of his mode of investigation, from which the following passages are extracted. It must be remembered that at the time he commenced the inquiry he was in the prime and vigor of intellectual life, being fifty-two years of age:

"It was in January, 1851, that I first began my investigations, and it was not until April, 1853, that I became a firm believer in the reality of spiritual intercourse. During twenty-three months of those twenty-seven, I witnessed several hundred manifestations in various forms. I kept very minute and careful records of many of them. My practice was, whenever I attended a circle, to keep in pencil a memorandum of all that took place, so far as I could, and, as soon as I returned home, to write out a full account of what I had wit-

nessed. I did all this with as much minuteness and particu-
larity as I had ever kept any record of a trial before me in
court. In this way, during that period, I preserved the record
of nearly two hundred interviews, running through some one
thousand six hundred pages of manuscript. I had these interviews with many different mediums, and under an infinite
variety of circumstances. No two interviews were alike.
There was always something new, or something different from
what had previously occurred; and it very seldom happened
that only the same persons were present. The manifestations
were of almost every known form, physical or mental; sometimes only one, and sometimes both combined.

"I resorted to every expedient I could devise to detect imposture and to guard against delusion. I felt in myself, and
saw in others, how exciting was the idea that we were actually communing with the dead; and I labored to prevent
any undue bias of my judgment. I was at times critical and
captious to an unreasonable extreme; and when my belief
was challenged, as it was over and over again, I refused to
yield, except to evidence that would leave no possible room
for cavil.

"I was severely exacting in my demands, and this would frequently happen. I would go to a circle with some doubt on
my mind as to the manifestations at the previous circle, and
something would happen aimed directly at that doubt, and
completely overthrowing it as it then seemed, so that I had
no longer any reason to doubt. But I would go home and
write out carefully my minutes of the evening, cogitate over
them for several days, compare them with previous records,
and finally find some loophole—some possibility that it might
have been something else than spiritual influence, and I would
go to the next circle with a new doubt, and a new set of
queries.

"I look back sometimes now, with a smile, at the ingenuity
I wasted in devising ways and means to avoid the possibility
of deception.

"It was a remarkable feature of my investigations that every
conceivable objection I could raise was, first or last, met and
answered."

The following extracts are from the "Appeal":

"I have seen a mahogany table, having a centre leg, and
with a lamp burning upon it, lifted from the floor at least a
foot, in spite of the efforts of those present, and shaken back-
ward and forward as one would shake a goblet in his hand,
and the lamp retain its place, though its glass pendants rang
again.

"I have known a mahogany chair thrown on its side and
moved swiftly back and forth on the floor, no one touching it,
through a room where there were at least a dozen people sitting, yet no one was touched; and it was repeatedly stopped
within a few inches of me, when it was coming with a violence which, if not arrested, must have broken my legs."

Having satisfied himself of the reality of the physical phenomena, he came to the question of whence comes the intelligence that was so remarkably connected with them. He says:

"Preparatory to meeting a circle, I have sat down alone in my room, and carefully prepared a series of questions to be propounded, and I have been surprised to find my questions answered, and in the precise order in which I wrote them, without my even taking my memorandum out of my pocket, and when not a person present knew that I had prepared questions, much less what they were. My most secret thoughts, those which I have never uttered to mortal man or woman, have been freely spoken to as if I had uttered them; and I have been admonished that my every thought was known to, and could be disclosed by, the intelligence which was thus manifesting itself.

"Still the question occurred, 'May not all this have been, by some mysterious operation, the mere reflex of the mind of some one present?' The answer was, that facts were communicated which were unknown then, but afterwards found to be true; like this, for instance: when I was absent last winter in Central America, my friends in town heard of my whereabouts and of the state of my health several times; and on my return, by comparing their information with the entries in my journal, it was found to be invariably correct. So thoughts have been uttered on subjects not then in my mind and utterly at variance with my own notions. This has often happened to me and to others, so as fully to establish the fact that it was not our minds that gave forth or affected the communication."

These few extracts sufficiently show that the writer was aware of the possible sources of error in such an inquiry; and the details given in the letters prove that he was constantly on his guard against them. He himself and his daughter became mediums; so that he afterwards obtained personal confirmation of many of the phenomena by himself alone. But all the phenomena referred to in the letters and "Appeal" occurred to him in the presence of others, who testified to them as well, and thus removed the possibility that the phenomena were subjective.

We have yet to add a notice of what will be perhaps, to many persons, the most startling and convincing of all the Judge's experiences. His own daughter became a medium for speaking foreign languages of which she was totally ignorant. He says: "She knows no language but her own, and a little smattering of boarding-school French; yet she has spoken in nine or ten different tongues, often for an hour at a time, with the ease and fluency of a native. It is not unfrequent that foreigners converse with their spirit-friends through her in their own language." One of these cases must be given :

"One evening, when some twelve or fifteen persons were in my parlor, Mr. E. D. Green, an artist of this city, was shown in, accompanied by a gentleman whom he introduced as Mr. Evangelides, of Greece. Ere long a spirit spoke to him through Laura, in English, and said so many things to him that he identified him as a friend who had died at his house a few years before, but of whom none of us had ever heard. Occasionally, through Laura, the spirit would speak a word or a sentence in Greek, until Mr. E. inquired if he could be understood if he spoke Greek? The residue of the conversation for more than an hour was, on his part, entirely in Greek, and on hers sometimes in Greek and sometimes in English. At times Laura would not understand what was the idea conveyed either by her or him. At other times she would understand him, though he spoke in Greek, and herself while uttering Greek words."

Several other cases are mentioned, and it is stated that this lady has spoken Spanish, French, Greek, Italian, Portuguese, Latin, Hungarian and Indian ; and other languages which were unknown to any person present.

This is by no means an isolated case, but it is given as being on most unexceptionable authority. A man must know whether his own daughter has learnt, so as to speak fluently, eight languages besides her own, or not. Those who carry on the conversation must know whether the language is spoken or not ; and in several cases—as the Latin, Spanish, and Indian—the Judge himself understood the language. And the phenomenon is connected with Spiritualism by the speaking being in the name of, and purporting to come from, some deceased person, and the subject matter being characteristic of that person. Such a case as this, which has been published sixteen years, ought to have been noticed and explained by those who profess to enlighten the public on the subject of Spiritualism.

Our next example is one of the most recent, but at the same time one of the most useful, converts to the truths of Spiritualism. Dr. George Sexton, M. D., M. A., L.L. D., was for many years the coadjutor of Mr. Bradlaugh, and one of the most earnest and energetic of the secularist teachers. The celebrated Robert Owen first called his attention to the subject of Spiritualism about twenty years ago. He read books, he saw a good deal of the ordinary physical manifestations, but he always "suspected that the mediums played tricks, and that the whole affair was nothing but clever conjuring by means of concealed machinery." He gave several lectures against Spiritualism in the usual style of non-believers, dwelling much on the absurdity and triviality of the phenomena, and ridiculing the idea that they were the work of spirits. Then came another old friend and fellow-secularist, Mr. Turley, who, after investigating the subject for the purpose of exposing it, became a firm believer. Dr. Sexton laughed at this conversion, yet it made a deep impression on his mind. Ten years passed away, and his next important investigation was with the Davenport brothers ; and it will be well for those who sneer at these much-abused young men to take note of the following account of Dr. Sexton's proceedings with them, and especially of the fact that they cheerfully submitted to every test the doctor suggested. He tells us (in his lecture, "How I became a Spiritualist,") that he visited them again and again, trying in vain to find out the trick. Then, he says—

"My partner—Dr. Barker—and I invited the Brothers to our houses, and, in order to guard against anything like trickery, we requested them not to bring any ropes, instruments, or other apparatus ; all these we ourselves had determined to supply. Moreover, as there were four of them, viz., the two Brothers Davenport, Mr. Fay, and Dr. Ferguson, we suspected that the two who were not tied might really do all that was done.   We therefore requested only two to come. They unhesitatingly complied with all these requests.

"We formed a circle, consisting entirely of members of our own families and a few private friends, with the one bare exception of Mrs. Fay.   In the circle we all joined hands, and as Mrs. Fay sat at one end she had one of her hands free, while I had hold of the other.   Thinking that she might be able to assist with the hand that was thus free, I asked, as a favor, that I might be allowed to hold both her hands—a proposition which she at once agreed to.   Now, without entering here at all into what took place, suffice it to say that we bound the mediums with our own ropes, placed their feet upon sheets of writing paper, and drew lines around their boots, so that if they moved their feet it should be impossible for them to place them again in the same position ; we laid pence on their toes, sealed the ropes, and in every way took precautions against their moving.   On the occasion to which I now refer, Mr. Bradlaugh and Mr. Charles Watts were present ; and when Mr. Fay's coat had been taken off, the ropes still remaining on his hands, Mr. Bradlaugh requested that his coat might be placed on Mr. Fay, which was immediately done, the ropes still remaining fastened.   We got, on this occasion, all the phenomena that usually occurred in the presence of these extraordinary men, particulars of which I shall probably give on another occasion.   Dr. Barker became a believer in Spiritualism from the time that the Brothers visited at his house. I did not see that any proof had been given that disembodied spirits had any hand in producing the phenomena ; but I was convinced that no tricks had been played, and that, therefore, these extraordinary physical manifestations were the result of some occult force in Nature which I had no means of explaining in the present state of my knowledge. All the physical phenomena that I had seen now became clear to me ; they were not accomplished by trickery, as I had formerly supposed, but were the result of some undiscovered law of Nature, which it was the business of the man of science to use his utmost endeavors to discover."

While he was maintaining this ground, Spiritualists often asked him how he explained the intelligence that was manifested; and he invariably replied that he had not yet seen proofs of any intelligence other than what might be that of the medium or of some other persons present in the circle, adding, that as soon as he did see proofs of such intelligence he should become a Spiritualist. In this position he stood for many years, till he naturally believed he should never see cause to change his opinion. He continued the inquiry, however, and in 1865 began to hold séances at home ; but it was years before any mental phenomena occurred which were absolutely conclusive, although they were often of so startling a nature as would have satisfied any one less skeptical. At length, after fifteen years of enlightened skepticism—a skepticism not founded upon ignorance, but which refused to go one step beyond what the facts so diligently pursued absolutely demonstrated—the needful evidence came :

"The proofs that I did ultimately receive are, many of them, of a character that I cannot describe minutely to a public audience, nor indeed have I time to do so. Suffice it to say, that I got in my own house, in the absence of all mediums other than those members of my own family and intimate private friends in whom mediumistic powers became developed, evidence of an irresistible character that the communications came from deceased friends and relatives. Intelligence was again and again displayed which could not possibly have had any other origin than that which it professed to have. Facts were named known to no one in the circle, and left to be verified afterwards. The identity of the spirits communicating was proved in a hundred different ways. Our dear departed ones made themselves palpable both to feeling and to sight ; and the doctrine of spirit-communion was proved beyond the shadow of a doubt. I soon found myself in the position of Dr. Fenwick in Lord Lytton's 'Strange Story.' 'Do you believe,' asked the female attendant of Margrave, 'in that which you seek ?' 'I have no belief,' was the answer. 'True science has none; true science questions all things, and takes nothing on credit. It knows but three states of mind—denial, conviction, and the vast interval between the two, which is not belief, but the suspension of judgment.' This describes exactly the phases through which my mind has passed."

Since Dr. Sexton has become a Spiritualist he has been as energetic an advocate for its truths as he had been before for the negations of secularism. His experience and ability as a lecturer, with his long schooling in every form of manifestation, render him one of the most valuable promulgators of its teachings. He has also done excellent service in exposing the pretensions of those conjurers who profess to expose Spiritualism. This he does in the most practical way, not only by explaining how the professed imitations of spiritual manifestations are performed, but by actually performing them before his audience ; and at the same time pointing out the important differences between what these people do and what occurs at good séances. Any one who wishes to comprehend how Dr. Lynn, Messrs. Maskelyne and Cook, and Herr Dobler perform some of their most curious feats have only to read his lecture, entitled, "Spirit Mediums and Conjurers," before going to witness their entertainments. We can hardly believe that the man who does this, and who during fifteen years of observation and experiment held out against the spiritual theory, is one of those who, as Lord Amberley tells us, "fall a victim to the most patent frauds, and are imposed upon by jugglery of the most vulgar order "; or who, as viewed from Prof. Tyndall's high scientific standpoint, are in a frame of mind before which science is utterly powerless—"dupes beyond the reach of proof, who like to believe and do not like to be undeceived." These be brave words ; but we leave our readers to judge whether they come with a very good grace from men who have the most slender and inadequate knowledge of the subject they are criticising, and no knowledge at all of the long-continued and conscientious investigations of many who are included in their wholesale animadversions.

Yet one more witness to these marvelous phenomena we must bring before our readers—a trained and experienced physicist, who has experimented in his own laboratory, and has applied tests and measurements of the most rigid and conclusive character. When Mr. Crookes—the discoverer of the metal thallium, and a Fellow of the Royal Society—first announced that he was going to investigate so-called spiritual phenomena, many public writers were all approval; for the complaint had long been that men of science were not permitted by mediums to inquire too scrupulously into the facts. One expressed "profound satisfaction that the subject was about to be investigated by a man so well qualified"; another was "gratified to learn that the matter is now receiving the attention of cool and clear headed men of recognized position in science"; while a third declared that "no one could doubt Mr. Crookes's ability to conduct the investigation with rigid philosophical impartiality." But these expressions were evidently insincere, and were only meant to apply in case the result was in accordance with the writers' notions of what it ought to be. Of course, a "scientific investigation" would explode the whole thing. Had not Faraday exploded table-turning? They hailed Mr. Crookes as the Daniel come to judgment—as the prophet who would curse their enemy, Spiritualism, by detecting imposture and illusion. But when the judge, after a patient trial lasting several years, decided against them, and their accepted prophet blessed the hated thing as an undoubted truth, their tone changed; and they began to suspect the judge's ability, and to pick holes in the evidence on which he founded his judgment.

In Mr. Crookes's latest paper, published in the Quarterly Journal of Science for January last, we are informed that he has pursued the inquiry for four years; and besides attending séances elsewhere, has had the opportunity of making numerous experiments in his own house with the two remarkable mediums already referred to, Mr. D. D. Home and Miss Kate Fox. These experiments were almost exclusively made in the light, under conditions of his own arranging, and with his own friends as witnesses. Such phenomena as percussive sounds; alteration of the weight of bodies; the rising of heavy bodies in the air without contact by any one; the levitation of human beings; luminous appearances of various kinds; the appearance of hands which lift small objects, yet are not the hands of any one present; direct writing by a luminous detached hand or by the pencil alone; phantom forms and faces; and various mental phenomena—have all been tested so variously and so repeatedly that Mr. Crookes is thoroughly satisfied of their objective reality. These phenomena are given in outline in the paper above referred to, and they will be detailed in full in a volume now preparing. I will not, therefore, weary my readers by repeating them here, but will remark, that these experiments have a weight

as evidence vastly greater than would be due to them as rest-
ing on the testimony of any man of science, however distinguished, because they are, in almost every case, confirmations
of what previous witnesses in immense numbers have testified
to, in various places, and under various conditions, during
the last twenty years. In every other experimental inquiry,
without exception, confirmation of the facts of an earlier ob-
server is held to add so greatly to their value, that no one
treats them with the same incredulity with which he might
have received them the first time they were announced. And
when the confirmation has been repeated by three or four independent observers under favorable conditions, and there is
nothing but theory or negative evidence against them, the
facts are admitted—at least provisionally, and until disproved
by a greater weight of evidence or by discovering the exact
source of the fallacy of preceding observers.

But here, a totally different—a most unreasonable and a
most unphilosophical—course is pursued. Each fresh observation, confirming previous evidence, is treated as though it
were now put forth for the *first* time ; and fresh confirmation
is asked of it. And when this fresh and independent confirmation comes, yet more confirmation is asked for, and so on
without end. This is a very clever way to ignore and stifle a
new truth ; but the facts of Spiritualism are ubiquitous in
their occurrence and of so indisputable a nature, as to compel
conviction in every earnest inquirer. It thus happens that
although every fresh convert requires a large proportion of
the series of demonstrative facts to be reproduced before he
will give his assent to them, the number of such converts has
gone on steadily increasing for a quarter of a century. Clergymen of all sects, literary men and lawyers, physicians in
large numbers, men of science not a few, secularists, philosophical skeptics, pure materialists, all have become converts
through the overwhelming logic of the phenomena which
Spiritualism has brought before them. And what have we
per contra ? Neither science nor philosophy, neither skepticism nor religion, has ever yet in this quarter of a century
made one single convert from the ranks of Spiritualism ! This
being the case, and fully appreciating the amount of candor
and fairness, and knowledge of the subject, that has been exhibited by their opponents, is it to be wondered at that a large
proportion of Spiritualists are now profoundly indifferent to
the opinion of men of science, and would not go one step out
of their way to convince them ? They say, that the move-

3

ment is going on quite fast enough; that it is spreading by its own inherent force of truth, and slowly permeating all classes of society. It has thriven in spite of abuse and persecution, ridicule and argument, and will continue to thrive whether endorsed by great names or not. Men of science, like all others, are welcome to enter its ranks; but they must satisfy themselves by their own persevering researches, not expect to have its proofs laid before them. Their rejection of its truths is their own loss, but cannot in the slightest degree affect the progress of Spiritualism. The attacks and criticisms of the press are borne good-humoredly, and seldom excite other feelings than pity for the willful ignorance and contempt for the overwhelming presumption of their writers. Such are the sentiments that are continually expressed by Spiritualists; and it is as well, perhaps, that the outer world, to whom the literature of the movement is as much unknown as the Vedas, should be made acquainted with them.

Investigation by the Dialectical Committee.—There are many other investigators who ought to be noticed in any complete sketch of the subject, but we have now only space to allude briefly to the "Report of the Committee of the Dialectical Society." Of this committee, consisting of thirty-three acting members, only eight were, at the commencement, believers in the reality of the phenomena, while not more than four accepted the spiritual theory. During the course of the inquiry at least twelve of the complete skeptics became convinced of the reality of many of the physical phenomena through attending the experimental sub-committees, and almost wholly by means of the mediumship of members of the committee. At least three members who were previously skeptics pursued their investigations outside the committee meetings, and in consequence have become thorough Spiritualists. My own observation as a member of the committee and of the largest and most active sub-committee, enables me to state that the degree of conviction produced in the minds of the various members was, allowing for marked differences of character, approximately proportionate to the amount of time and care bestowed on the investigation. This fact, which is what occurs in all investigation into these phenomena, is a characteristic result of the examination into any natural phenomena. The examination into an imposture or delusion has, invariably, exactly opposite results: those who have slender experience being deceived, while those who perseveringly continue the inquiry inevitably find out the source of the deception or the delusion. If this were not so, the discovery of truth and the detection of error would be alike impossible. The result of this inquiry on the members of the committee themselves is, therefore, of more importance than the actual phenomena they witnessed, since these were far less striking than many of the facts already mentioned. But they are also of importance as confirming, by a body of intelligent and unprejudiced men, the results obtained by previous individual inquirers.

Before leaving this report, I must call attention to the evidence it furnishes of the state of opinion among men of education in France. M. Camille Flammarion, the well-known astronomer, sent a communication to the committee which deserves special consideration. Besides declaring his own acceptance of the objective reality of the phenomena after ten years of investigation, he makes the following statement:

"My learned teacher and friend, M. Babinet, of the Institute, who has endeavored, with M. E. Liais (now Director of the Observatory of Brazil), and several others of my colleagues of the Observatory of Paris, to ascertain their nature and cause, is not fully convinced of the intervention of spirits in their production ; though this hypothesis, by which alone certain categories of these phenomena would seem to be explicable, has been adopted by many of our most esteemed *savants*, among others by Dr. Hœffle, the learned author of the 'History of Chemistry,' and the 'General Encyclopædia'; and by the diligent laborer in the field of astronomic discovery whose death we have recently had to deplore, M. Hermann Goldschmidt, the discoverer of fourteen planets."

It thus appears that in France, as well as in America and in this country, men of science of no mean rank have investigated these phenomena and have found them to be realities ; while some of the most eminent hold the spiritual theory to be the only one that will explain them.

This seems the proper place to notice the astounding assertion of certain writers, that there is not "a particle of evidence" to support the spiritual theory; that those who accept it betray "hopeless inability to discriminate between adequate and inadequate proof of facts" ; that the theory is "formed apart from facts"; and that those who accept it are so unable to reason as to "jump to the conclusion" that it must be spirits that move tables, merely because they do not know how else they can be moved. The preceding account of how converts to Spiritualism have been made is a sufficient answer to all this ignorant assertion. The spiritual theory,

as a rule, has only been adopted as a last resource, when all
other theories have hopelessly broken down ; and when fact
after fact, phenomenon after phenomenon, has presented
itself, giving direct proof that the so-called dead are still
alive. The spiritual theory is the logical outcome of the
whole of the facts. Those who deny it, in every instance
with which I am acquainted, either from ignorance or disbelief, leave half the facts out of view. Take the one case
(out of many almost equally conclusive) of Mr. Livermore,
who, during five years, on hundreds of occasions, saw, felt
and heard the movements of the figure of his dead wife in
absolute, unmistakable, living form—a form which could
move objects, and which repeatedly wrote to him in her
own handwriting and her own language, on cards which re-
mained after the figure had disappeared ; a form which was
equally visible and tangible to two friends ; which appeared in his own house, in a room absolutely secured, with
the presence of only a young girl, the medium. Had these
three men "not a particle of evidence" for the spiritual theory ? Is it, in fact, possible to conceive or suggest any more
complete proof ?   The facts must be got rid of before you can
abolish the theory ; and simple denial or disbelief does not
get rid of facts testified during a space of five years by three
witnesses, all men in responsible positions, and carrying on
their affairs during the whole period in a manner to win the
respect and confidence of their fellow-citizens.*

---

* The objection will here inevitably be made : "These wonderful things
always happen in America. When they occur in England it will be time
enough to inquire into them." Singularly enough, after this article was
in the press the final test was obtained, which demonstrated the occurrence of similar phenomena in London. A short statement may, therefore, be interesting for those who cannot digest American evidence. For
some years a young lady, Miss Florence Cook, has exhibited remarkable
mediumship, which latterly culminated in the production of an entire female form purporting to be spiritual, and which appeared barefooted and
in white flowing robes while she lay entranced, in dark clothing and securely bound, in a cabinet or adjacent room. Notwithstanding that tests
of an apparently conclusive character were employed, many visitors,
Spiritualists as well as skeptics, got the impression that all was not as it
shou'd be; owing, in part, to the resemblance of the supposed spirit to
Miss Cook, and also to the fact that the two could not be seen at the same
time. Some supposed that Miss C. was an impostor, who managed to con-
ceal a white robe about her (although she was often searched), and who,
although she was securely tied with tapes and sealed, was able to get out
of her bonds, dress and undress herself, and get into them again, all in
the dark, and in so complete and skillful a manner as to defy detection.
Others thought that the spirit released her, provided her with a white
dress, and sent her forth to personate a ghost. The belief that there was
something wrong led one gentleman—an ardent Spiritualist—to seize the
supposed spirit and endeavor to hold it, in the hope that some other person
would open the cabinet-door and see if Miss Cook was really there. This
was, unfortunately, not done; but the great resemblance of the being he
seized to Miss Cook, its perfect solidity, and the vigorous struggles it
made to escape from him, convinced this gentleman that it was Miss Cook
herself, although the rest of the company, a few minutes afterwards,

SPIRIT PHOTOGRAPHS.

We now approach a subject which cannot be omitted in any impartial sketch of the evidences of Spiritualism, since it is that which furnishes perhaps the most unassailable demonstration it is possible to obtain, of the objective reality of spiritual forms, and also of the truthful nature of the evidence furnished by seers when they describe figures visible to themselves alone. It has been already indicated—and it is a fact, of which the records of Spiritualism furnish ample proof—that different individuals possess the power of seeing such forms and figures in very variable degrees. Thus, it often happens at a séance, that some will see distinct lights of which they will describe the form, appearance and position, while others see nothing at all. If only one or two persons see the lights, the rest will naturally impute it to their imagination ; but there are cases in which only one or two of those present are unable to see them. There are also cases in which all see them, but in very different degrees of distinctness ; yet that they see the same objects is proved by their all agreeing as to the position and the movement of the lights. Again, what some see as merely luminous clouds, others will see as distinct

---

found her bound and sealed just as she had been left an hour before. To determine the question conclusively, experiments have been made within the last few weeks by two scientific men. Mr. C. F. Varley, F.R.S., the eminent electrician, made use of a galvanic battery and cable-testing apparatus, and passed a current through Miss Cook's body (by fastening sovereigns soldered to wires to her arms). The apparatus was so delicate that any movement whatever was instantly indicated, while it was impossible for the young lady to dress and act as a ghost without breaking the circuit. Yet under these conditions the spirit-form did appear, exhibited its arms, spoke, wrote, and touched several persons; and this happened. be it remembered, not in the medium's own house, but in that of a private gentleman in the West End of London. For nearly an hour the circuit was never broken, and at the conclusion Miss Cook was found in a deep trance. Since this remarkable experiment Mr. William Crookes, F.R.S., has obtained, if possible, still more satisfactory evidence. He contrived a phosphorus lamp, and, armed with this, was allowed to go into the dark room accompanied by the spirit, and there saw and felt Miss Cook, dressed in black velvet, lying in a trance on the floor, while the spirit-form, in white robes, stood close beside her. During the evening this spirit-form had been for nearly an hour walking and talking with the company; and Mr. Crookes, by permission, clasped the figure in his arms, and found it to be, apparently, a real living woman, just as the skeptical gentleman had done. Yet this figure is not that of Miss Cook, nor of any other human being, since it appeared and disappeared in Mr. Crookes's own house as completely as in that of the medium herself. The full statements of Messrs. Varley and Crookes, with a mass of interesting detail on the subject, appeared in the "Spiritualist" newspaper in March and April last; and they serve to show that whatever marvels occur in America can be reproduced here, and that men of science are not precluded from investigating these phenomena with scientific instruments and by scientific methods. In the concluding part of this paper we shall be able to show that another class of manifestatation which originated in America—that of the so-called spirit-photographs—has been first critically examined and completely demonstrated in our own country.

human forms, either partial or entire. In other cases all present see the form—whether hand, face, or entire figure—with equal distinctness. Again, the objective reality of these appearances is sometimes proved by their being touched, or by their being seen to move objects—in some cases heard to speak, in others seen to write, by several persons at one and the same time; the figure seen or the writing produced being sometimes unmistakably recognizable as that of some deceased friend. A volume could easily be filled with records of this class of appearances, authenticated by place, date, and names of witnesses; and a considerable selection is to be found in the works of Mr. Robert Dale Owen.

Now, at this point, an inquirer, who had not pre-judged the question, and who did not believe his own knowledge of the universe to be so complete as to justify him in rejecting all evidence for facts which he had hitherto considered to be in the highest degree improbable, might fairly say, "Your evidence for the appearance of visible, tangible, spiritual forms, is very strong; but I should like to have them submitted to a crucial test, which would quite settle the question of the possibility of their being due to a coincident delusion of several senses of several persons at the same time; and, if satisfactory, would demonstrate their objective reality in a way nothing else can do. If they really reflect or emit light which makes them visible to human eyes, *they can be photographed.* Photograph them, and you will have an unanswerable proof that your human witnesses are trustworthy." Two years ago we could only have replied to this very proper suggestion, that we believed it had been done and could be again done, but that we had no satisfactory evidence to offer. Now, however, we are in a position to state, not only that it has been frequently done, but that the evidence is of such a nature as to satisfy any one who will take the trouble carefully to examine it. This evidence we will now lay before our readers, and we venture to think they will acknowledge it to be most remarkable.

Before doing so it may be as well to clear away a popular misconception. Mr. Lewes advised the Dialectical Committee to distinguish carefully between "facts and inferences from facts." This is especially necessary in the case of what are called spirit photographs. The figures which occur in these, when not produced by any human agency, may be of "spiritual" origin, without being figures "of spirits." There is much evidence to show that they are, in some cases, forms produced by invisible intelligences, but distinct from them.

In other cases the intelligence appears to clothe itself with matter capable of being perceived by us ; but even then it does not follow that the form produced is the actual image of the spiritual form. It may be but a reproduction of the former mortal form with its terrestrial accompaniments, *for purposes of recognition.*

Most persons have heard of these "ghost-pictures," and how easily they can be made to order by any photographer, and are therefore disposed to think they can be of no use as evidence. But a little consideration will show them that the means by which sham ghosts can be manufactured being so well known to all photographers, it becomes easy to apply tests or arrange conditions so as to prevent imposition. The following are some of the more obvious :

1. If a person with a knowledge of photography takes his own glass plates, examines the camera used and all the accessories, and watches the whole process of taking a picture, then, if any definite form appears on the negative besides the sitter, it is a proof that some object was present capable of reflecting or emitting the actinic rays, although invisible to those present. 2. If an unmistakable likeness appears of a deceased person totally unknown to the photographer. 3. If figures appear on the negative having a definite relation to the figure of the sitter, who chooses his own position, attitude and accompaniments, it is a proof that invisible figures were really there. 4. If a figure appears draped in white, and partly behind the dark body of the sitter without in the least showing through, it is a proof that the white figure was there at the same time, because the dark parts of the negative are transparent, and any white picture in any way superposed would show through. 5. Even should none of these tests be applied, yet if a medium, quite independent of the photographer, sees and describes a figure during the sitting and an exactly corresponding figure appears on the plate, it is a proof that such a figure was there.

Every one of these tests have now been successfully applied in our own country, as the following outline of the facts will show :

The accounts of spirit-photography in several parts of the United States caused many Spiritualists in this country to make experiments ; but for a long time without success. Mr. and Mrs. Guppy, who are both amateur photographers, tried at their own house, and failed. In March, 1872, they went one day to Mr. Hudson's, a photographer living near them

(not a Spiritualist), to get some *cartes de visite* of Mrs. Guppy.
After the sitting the idea suddenly struck Mr. Guppy that he
would try for a spirit-photograph. He sat down, told Mrs.
G. to go behind the background, and had a picture taken.
There came out behind him a large, indefinite, oval white
patch, somewhat resembling the outline of a draped figure.
Mrs. Guppy, behind the background, was dressed in black.

This is the first spirit-photograph taken in England, and it
is perhaps more satisfactory on account of the suddenness of
the impulse under which it was taken, and the great white
patch which no impostor would have attempted to produce,
and which, taken by itself, utterly spoils the picture. A few
days afterwards, Mr. and Mrs. Guppy and their little boy
went without any notice. Mrs. Guppy sat on the ground
holding the boy on a stool. Her husband stood behind looking on. The picture thus produced is most remarkable. A
tall female figure, finely draped in white, gauzy robes, stands
directly behind and above the sitters, looking down on them
and holding its open hands over their heads, as if giving a
benediction. The face is somewhat Eastern, and, with the
hands, is beautifully defined. The white robes pass behind
the sitters' dark figures without in the least showing through.
A second picture was then taken as soon as a plate could be
prepared ; and it was fortunate it was so, for it resulted in a
most remarkable test. Mrs. Guppy again knelt with the boy ;
but this time she did not stoop so much, and her head was
higher. The same white figure comes out equally well defined, but *it has changed its position in a manner exactly corresponding to the slight change of Mrs. Guppy's position.* The
hands were before on a level ; now one is raised considerably
higher than the other, so as to keep it about the same distance
from Mrs. Guppy's head as it was before. The folds of the
drapery all correspondingly differ, and the head is slightly
turned. Here, then, one of two things is absolutely certain.
Either there was a living, intelligent, but invisible being
present, or Mr. and Mrs. Guppy, the photographer, and some
fourth person, planned a wicked imposture, and have main-
tained it ever since. Knowing Mr. and Mrs. Guppy so well
as I do, I feel an absolute conviction that they are as incapable of an imposture of this kind as any earnest inquirer after
truth in the department of natural science.

The report of these pictures soon spread. Spiritualists in
great numbers came to try for similar results, with varying
degrees of success ; till after a time rumor of imposture arose,

and it is now firmly believed by many, from suspicious appearances on the pictures and from other circumstances, that a large number of shams have been produced. It is certainly not to be wondered at if it be so. The photographer, remember, was not a Spiritualist, and was utterly puzzled at the pictures above described. Scores of persons came to him, and he saw that they were satisfied if they got a second figure with themselves, and dissatisfied if they did not. He *may* have made arrangements by which to satisfy everybody. One thing is clear: that if there has been imposture, it was at once detected by Spiritualists themselves ; if not, then Spiritualists have been quick in noticing what appeared to indicate it. Those, however, who most strongly assert imposture, allow that a large number of genuine pictures have been taken. But, true or not, the cry of imposture did good, since it showed the necessity for tests and for independent confirmation of the facts.

The test of clearly recognizable likenesses of deceased friends has often been obtained. Mr. William Howitt, who went without previous notice, obtained likenesses of two sons, many years dead, and of the very existence of one of which even the friend who accompanied Mr. Howitt was ignorant. The likenesses were instantly recognized by Mrs. Howitt ; and Mr. Howitt declares them to be "perfect and unmistakable." (Spiritual Magazine, Oct., 1872.) Dr. Thomson, of Clifton, obtained a photograph of himself, accompanied by that of a lady he did not know. He sent it to his uncle in Scotland, simply asking if he recognized a resemblance to any of the family deceased. The reply was that it was the likeness of Dr. Thomson's own mother, who died at his birth ; and there being no picture of her in existence, he had no idea what she was like. The uncle very naturally remarked, that he "could not understand how it was done." (Spiritual Magazine, Oct., 1873.) Many other instances of recognition have occurred, but I will only add my personal testimony. A few weeks back I myself went to the same photographer's for the first time, and obtained a most unmistakable likeness of a deceased relative. We will now pass to a better class of evidence, the private experiments of amateurs.

Mr. Thomas Slater, an old-established optician in the Euston Road, and an amateur photographer, took with him to Mr. Hudson's a new camera of his own manufacture and his own glasses, saw everything done, and obtained a portrait with a second figure on it. He then began experimenting in his own private house, and during last summer obtained some remarkable results. The first of his successes contains two heads by the side of a portrait of his sister. One of these heads is unmistakably the late Lord Brougham's; the other, much less distinct, is recognized by Mr. Slater as that of Robert Owen, whom he knew intimately up to the time of his death. He has since obtained several excellent pictures of the same class. One in particular shows a female in black and white flowing robes, standing by the side of Mr. Slater. In another the head and bust appears, leaning over his shoulder. The faces of these two are much alike, and other members of the family recognize them as likenesses of Mr. Slater's mother, who died when he was an infant. In another a pretty child-figure, also draped, stands beside Mr. Slater's little boy. Now, whether these figures are correctly identified or not, is not the essential point. The fact that *any* figures, so clear and unmistakably human in appearance as these, should appear on plates taken in his own private studio by an experienced optician and amateur photographer, who makes all his apparatus himself, and with no one present but the members of his own family, is the real marvel. In one case a second figure appeared on a plate with himself, taken by Mr. Slater when he was absolutely alone—by the simple process of occupying the sitter's chair after uncapping the camera. He and his family being themselves mediums, they require no extraneous assistance; and this may perhaps be the reason why he has succeeded so well. One of the most extraordinary pictures obtained by Mr. Slater is a full-length portrait of his sister, in which there is no second figure, but the sitter appears covered all over with a kind of transparent lace drapery, which on examination is seen to be wholly made up of shaded circles of different sizes, quite unlike any material fabric I have seen or heard of.

Mr. Slater has himself shown me all these pictures and explained the conditions under which they were produced. That they are not impostures is certain ; and as the first independent confirmations of what had been previously obtained only through professional photographers, their value is inestimable.

A less successful but not perhaps on that account less satisfactory confirmation has been obtained by another amateur, who, after eighteen months of experiment, obtained a partial success. Mr. R. Williams, M. A., Ph. D., of Hayward's

Heath, succeeded last summer in obtaining three photographs, each with part of a human form besides the sitter, one
having the features distinctly marked. Subsequently another was obtained, with a well-formed figure of a man standing
at the side of the sitter, but while being developed, this figure faded away entirely. Mr. Williams assures me (in a letter) that in these experiments there was "no room for trick
or for the production of these figures by any known means."

The editor of the British Journal of Photography has made
experiments at Mr. Hudson's studio, taking his own collodion
and new plates, and doing everything himself, yet there were
"abnormal appearances" on the pictures, although no distinct
figures.

We now come to the valuable and conclusive experiments
of Mr. John Beattie, of Clifton, a retired photographer of
twenty years' experience, and of whom the above-mentioned
editor says : " Every one who knows Mr. Beattie will give
him credit for being a thoughtful, skillful, and intelligent
photographer, one of the last men in the world to be easily
deceived, at least in matters relating to photography, and one
quite incapable of deceiving others."

Mr. Beattie has been assisted in his researches by Dr. Thomson, an Edinburgh M. D., who has practiced photography, as
an amateur, for twenty-five years. They experimented at
the studio of a friend, who was not a Spiritualist (but who
became a medium during the experiments), and had the ser-
vices of a tradesman—with whom they were well acquainted
—as a medium. The whole of the photographic work was
done by Messrs Beattie and Thomson, the other two sitting
at a small table. The pictures were taken in series of three,
within a few seconds of each other, and several of these series were taken at each sitting. The figures produced are,
for the most part, not human, but variously-formed and shaded white patches, which in successive pictures change their
form, and develop, as it were, into a more perfect or complete
type. Thus, one set of five begins with two white somewhat
angular patches over the middle sitter, and ends with a rude
but unmistakable white female figure, covering the larger part
of the plate. The other three show intermediate states, indi-
cating a continuous change of form from the first figure to
the last. Another set (of four pictures) begins with a white
vertical cylinder over the body of the medium, and a shorter
one on his head. These change their form in the second and
third, and in the last become laterally spread out into lumi-

nous masses resembling nebulæ. Another set of three is very curious. The first has an oblique flowing luminous patch from the table to the ground ; in the second, this has changed to a white serpentine column, ending in a point above the medium's head ; in the third, the column has become broader and somewhat double, with the curve in an opposite direction, and with a head-like termination. The change of the curvature may have some connection with a change in the position of the sitters, which is seen to have taken place between the second and the third of this set. There are two others, taken, like all the preceding, in 1872, but which the medium described during the exposure. The first, he said, was a thick white fog ; and the picture came out all shaded white, with not a trace of any of the sitters. The other was described as a fog with a figure standing in it; and here a white human figure is alone seen in the almost uniform foggy surface. During the experiments made in 1873, the medium, *in every case*, minutely and correctly described the appearances which afterwards came out on the plate. In one there is a luminous-rayed star of large size, with a human face faintly visible in the centre. This is the last of three in which the star developed, and the whole were accurately described by the medium. In another set of three, the medium first described "a light behind him, coming from the floor." The next, "a light rising over another person's arms, coming from his own boot." The third, "there is the same light, but now a column comes up through the table, and it is hot to my hands." Then he suddenly exclaimed, "What a bright light up there! Can you not see it?" pointing to it with his hand. All this most accurately describes the three pictures, and in the last, the medium's hand is seen pointing to a white patch which appears overhead. There are other curious developments, the nature of which is already sufficiently indicated ; but one very startling single picture must be mentioned. During the exposure one medium said he saw on the background a black figure, the other medium saw a light figure by the side of the black one. In the picture both these figures appear, the light one very faintly, the black one much more distinctly, of a gigantic size, with a massive coarse-featured face and long hair.—(*Spiritual Magazine, January and August,* 1873; *Photographic News, June* 28*th,* 1872.)

Mr. Beattie has been so good as to send me for examination a complete set of these most extraordinary photographs, thirty-two in number, and has furnished me with any particulars

I desired. I have described them as correctly as I am able ;
and Dr. Thomson has authorized me to use his name as confirming Mr. Beattie's account of the conditions under which
they appeared. These experiments were not made without
labor and perseverance. Sometimes twenty consecutive pictures produced absolutely nothing unusual. Hundreds have
been taken, and more than half have been complete failures.
But the successes have been well worth the labor. They
demonstrate the fact that what a medium or sensitive sees
(even where no one else sees anything) may often have an
objective existence. They teach us that perhaps the book-
seller, Nicolai, of Berlin—whose case has been quoted *ad nau-
seam* as the type of a "spectral illusion"—saw real beings
after all ; and that, had photography been then discovered
and properly applied, we might now have the portraits of the
invisible men and women who crowded his room. They give
us hints of a process by which the figures seen at séances may
have to be gradually formed or developed, and enable us better to understand the statements repeatedly made by the
communicating intelligences, that it is very difficult to produce definite, visible and tangible forms, and that it can only
be done under a rare combination of favorable conditions.

We find, then, that three amateur photographers, working
independently in different parts of England, separately confirm the fact of spirit-photography—already demonstrated to
the satisfaction of many who had tested it through professional photographers. The experiments of Mr. Beattie and Dr.
Thomson are alone absolutely conclusive ; and, taken in connection with those of Mr. Slater and Dr. Williams, and the
test photographs, like those of Mrs. Guppy, establish as a
scientific fact the objective existence of invisible human
forms and definite invisible actinic images. Before leaving
the photographic phenomena we have to notice two curious
points in connection with them. The actinic action of the
spirit-forms is peculiar, and much more rapid than that of
the light reflected from ordinary material forms ; for the
figures start out the moment the developing fluid touches
them, while the figure of the sitter appears much later. Mr.
Beattie noticed this throughout his experiments, and I was
myself much struck with it when watching the development
of three pictures recently taken at Mr. Hudson's. The second figure, though by no means bright, always came out long
before any other part of the picture. The other singular
thing is, the copious drapery in which these forms are almost

always enveloped, so as to show only just what is necessary
for recognition of the face and figure. The explanation
given of this is, that the human form is more difficult to ma-
terialize than drapery. The conventional "white-sheeted
ghost" was not then all fancy, but had a foundation in fact—
a fact, too, of deep significance, dependent on the laws of a
yet unknown chemistry.

SUMMARY OF THE MORE IMPORTANT MANI-
FESTATIONS, PHYSICAL AND MENTAL.

As we have not been able to give an account of many curious facts which occur with the various classes of mediums,
the following catalogue of the more important and well-char-
actorized phenomena may be useful. They may be grouped
provisionally, as, Physical, or those in which material objects
are acted on, or apparently material bodies produced ; and
Mental, or those which consist in the exhibition, by the medium, of powers or faculties not possessed in the normal state.
The principal physical phenomena are the following :
1. *Simple Physical Phenomena.*—Producing sounds of all
kinds, from a delicate tick to blows like those of a heavy
sledge-hammer. Altering the weight of bodies. Moving
bodies without human agency. Raising bodies into the air.
Conveying bodies to a distance out of and into closed rooms.
Releasing mediums from every description of bonds, even
from welded iron rings, as has happened in America.
2. *Chemical.*—Preserving from the effects of fire, as already
detailed.
3. *Direct Writing and Drawing.*—Producing writing or
drawing on marked papers, placed in such positions that no
human hand (or foot) can touch them. Sometimes, visibly
to the spectators, a pencil rising up and writing or drawing
apparently by itself. Some of the drawings in many colors
have been produced on marked paper in from ten to twenty
seconds, and the colors found wet. (See Mr. Coleman's evidence in "Dialectical Report," p. 143, confirmed by Lord
Borthwick, p. 150.) Mr. Thomas Slater, of 136 Euston Road,
is now obtaining communication in the following manner : A
bit of slate pencil an eighth of an inch long is laid on a table ; a clean slate is laid over this, in a well-lighted room ; the
sound of writing is then heard, and in a few minutes a communication of considerable length is found distinctly written.

At other times the slate is held between himself and another person, their other hands being joined. Some of these communications are philosophical discussions on the nature of spirit and matter, supporting the usual Spiritual theory on this subject.

4. *Musical Phenomena.*—Musical instruments, of various kinds, played without human agency, from a hand-bell to a closed piano. With some mediums, and where the conditions are favorable, original musical compositions of a very high character are produced. This occurs with Mr. Home.

5. *Spiritual Forms.*—These are either luminous appearances, sparks, stars, globes of light, luminous clouds, &c.; or, hands, faces, or entire human figures, usually covered with flowing drapery, except a portion of the face and hands. The human forms are often capable of moving solid objects, and are both visible and tangible to all present. In other cases they are only visible to seers, but when this is the case it sometimes happens that the seer describes the figure as lifting a flower or a pen, and others present see the flower or the pen apparently move by itself. In some cases they speak distinctly; in others the voice is heard by all, the form only seen by the medium. The flowing robes of these forms have in some cases been examined, and pieces cut off, which have in a short time melted away. Flowers are also brought, some of which fade away and vanish; others are real, and can be kept indefinitely. It must not be concluded that any of these forms are actual spirits; they are probably only temporary forms produced by spirits for purposes of test, or of recognition by their friends. This is the account invariably given of them by communications obtained in various ways; so that the objection once thought to be so crushing—that there can be no "ghosts" of clothes, armor, or walking-sticks—ceases to have any weight.

6. *Spiritual Photographs.*—These, as just detailed, demonstrate by a purely physical experiment the trustworthiness of the preceding class of observations.

We now come to the mental phenomena, of which the following are the chief :

1. *Automatic Writing.*—The medium writes involuntarily ; often matter which he is not thinking about, does not expect, and does not like. Occasionally definite and correct information is given of facts of which the medium has not, nor ever had, any knowledge. Sometimes future events are accurately predicted. The writing takes place either by the hand or

through a planchette. Often the handwriting changes. Sometimes it is written backwards; sometimes in languages the
medium does not understand.

2. *Seeing, or Clairvoyance and Clairaudience.*—This is of
various kinds. Some mediums see the forms of deceased persons unknown to them, and describe their peculiarities so
minutely that their friends at once recognize them. They
often hear voices, through which they obtain names, date,
and place, connected with the individuals so described. Others read sealed letters in any language, and write appropriate
answers.

3. *Trance-Speaking.*—The medium goes into a more or less
unconscious state, and then speaks, often on matters and in a
style far beyond his own capacities. Thus, Serjeant Cox—
no mean judge on a matter of literary style—says, "I have
heard an uneducated bar-man, when in a state of trance,
maintain a dialogue with a party of philosophers on 'Reason
and Foreknowledge, Will and Fate,' and hold his own against
them. I have put to him the most difficult questions in psy-
chology, and received answers, always thoughtful, often full
of wisdom, and invariably conveyed in choice and elegant
language. Nevertheless a quarter of an hour afterwards,
when released from the trance, he was unable to answer the
simplest query on a philosophical subject, and was even at a
loss for sufficient language to express a commonplace idea,"
("What am I?" Vol. II., p. 242.) That this is not overstated
I can myself testify, from repeated observation of the same
medium. And from other trance-speakers—such as Mrs.
Hardinge, Mrs. Tappan, and Mr. Peebles—I have heard
discourses which, for high and sustained eloquence, noble
thoughts, and high moral purpose, surpassed the best efforts
of any preacher or lecturer within my experience.

4. *Impersonation.*—This occurs during trance. The medium
seems taken possession of by another being; speaks, looks
and acts the character in a most marvelous manner; in some
cases speaks foreign languages never even heard in the normal state; as in the case of Miss Edmonds, already given.
When the influence is violent or painful, the effects are such
as have been in all ages imputed to possession by evil spirits.

5. *Healing.*—There are various forms of this. Sometimes
by mere laying on of hands, an exalted form of simple mes-
meric healing. Sometimes, in the trance state, the medium at
once discovers the hidden malady, and prescribes for it, often
describing very exactly the morbid appearance of internal
organs.

The purely mental phenomena are generally of no use as evidence to non-Spiritualists, except in those few cases where rigid tests can be applied; but they are so intimately connected with the physical series, and often so interwoven with them, that no one who has sufficient experience to satisfy him of the reality of the former, fails to see that the latter form part of the general system, and are dependent on the same agencies.

With the physical series the case is very different. They form a connected body of evidence, from the simplest to the most complex and astounding, every single component fact of which can be and has been repeatedly demonstrated by itself; while each gives weight and confirmation to all the rest. They have all, or nearly all, been before the world for twenty years; the theories and explanations of reviewers and critics do not touch them, or in any way satisfy any sane man who has repeatedly witnessed them; they have been tested and examined by skeptics of every grade of incredulity, men in every way qualified to detect imposture or to discover natural causes—trained physicists, medical men, lawyers and men of business—but in every case the investigators have either retired baffled, or become converts.

There have, it is true, been some impostors who have attempted to imitate the phenomena; but such cases are few in number, and have been discovered by tests far less severe than those to which the genuine phenomena have been submitted over and over again; and a large proportion of these phenomena have never been imitated, because they are beyond successful imitation.

Now what do our leaders of public opinion say, when a scientific man of proved ability again observes a large portion of the more extraordinary phenomena, in his own house, under test conditions, and affirms their objective reality; and this not after a hasty examination, but after four years of research? Men "with heavy scientific appendages to their names" refuse to examine them when invited; the eminent society of which he is a fellow refuses to record them; and the press cries out that it wants better witnesses than Mr. Crookes, and that such facts want "confirmation" before they can be believed. But why more confirmation? And when again "confirmed," who is to confirm the confirmer? After the whole range of the phenomena had been before the world ten years, and had convinced skeptics by tens of thousands—skeptics, be it remembered, of common sense and more

4

than common acuteness, Americans of all classes—they were *confirmed* by the first chemist in America, Professor Robert Hare. Two years later they were again confirmed by the elaborate and persevering inquiries of one of the first American lawyers, Judge Edmonds. Then by another good chemist, Professor Mapes. In France the truth of the simpler physical phenomena was *confirmed* by Count A. de Gasparin, in 1854; and since then French astronomers, mathematicians and chemists of high rank have *confirmed* them. Professor Thury of Geneva again *confirmed* them, in 1855. In our own country such men as Professor de Morgan, Dr. Lockhart Robertson, T. Adolphus Trollope, Dr. Robert Chambers, Serjeant Cox, Mr. C. F. Varley, as well as the skeptical Dialectical Committee, have independently *confirmed* large portions of them; and lastly comes Mr. William Crookes, F.R.S., with four years of research and unrestricted experiment with the two oldest and most remarkable mediums in the world, and again *confirms* almost the whole series! But even this is not all. Through an independent set of most competent observers we have the crucial test of photography; a witness which cannot be deceived, which has no preconceived opinions, which cannot register "subjective" impressions; a thoroughly scientific witness, who is admitted into our law courts, and whose testimony is good as against any number of recollections of what did happen or opinions as to what ought to and must have happened. And what have the other side brought against this overwhelming array of consistent and unimpeachable evidence? They have merely made absurd and inadequate suppositions, but have not disproved or explained away one weighty fact!

My position, therefore, is, that the phenomena of Spiritualism in their entirety do *not* require further confirmation. They are proved quite as well as any facts are proved in other sciences; and it is not denial or quibbling that can disprove any of them, but only fresh facts and accurate deductions from those facts. When the opponents of Spiritualism can give a record of their researches approaching in duration and completeness to those of its advocates; and when they can discover and show in detail, either how the phenomena are produced or how the many sane and able men here referred to have been deluded into a coincident belief that they have witnessed them: and when they can prove the correctness of their theory by producing a like belief in a body of equally sane and able unbelievers—then, and not till then,

will it be necessary for Spiritualists to produce fresh confirmation of facts which are, and always have been, sufficiently real and indisputable to satisfy any honest and persevering
inquirer.

This being the state of the case as regards evidence and
proof, we are fully justified in taking the *facts* of Modern
Spiritualism (and with them the spiritual theory as the only
tenable one) as being fully established. It only remains to
give a brief account of the more important uses and teachings
of Spiritualism.

HISTORICAL TEACHINGS OF SPIRITUALISM.

The lessons which Modern Spiritualism teaches may be
classed under two heads. In the first place, we find that it
gives a rational account of various phenomena in human history which physical science has been unable to explain, and
has therefore rejected or ignored ; and, in the second, we derive
from it some definite information as to man's nature and destiny, and, founded on this, an ethical system of great practical
efficacy. The following are some of the more important phenomena of history and of human nature which science cannot
deal with, but which Spiritualism explains :

1. It is no small thing that the Spiritualist finds himself
able to rehabilitate Socrates as a sane man, and his "demon"
as an intelligent spiritual being who accompanied him through
life—in other words, a guardian spirit. The non-Spiritualist
is obliged to look upon one of the greatest men in human history, not only as subject all his life to a mental illusion, but
as being so weak, foolish, or superstitious as never to discover that it was an illusion. He is obliged to disbelieve the fact
asserted by contemporaries and by Socrates himself, that it
forewarned him truly of dangers ; and to hold that this noble
man, this subtle reasoner, this religious skeptic, who was
looked up to with veneration and love by the great men who
were his pupils, was imposed upon by his own fancies, and
never during a long life found out that they were fancies, and
that their supposed monitions were as often wrong as right.
It is a positive mental relief not to have to think thus of Socrates.

2. Spiritualism allows us to believe that the oracles of antiquity were not all impostures ; that a whole people, perhaps
the most intellectually acute who ever existed, were not all

dupes. In discussing the question, "Why the Prophetess
Pythia giveth no Answers now from the Oracle in Verse,"
Plutarch tells us that when kings and states consulted the
oracle on weighty matters that might do harm if made public,
the replies were couched in enigmatical language; but when
private persons asked about their own affairs they got direct
answers in the plainest terms, so that some people even com-
plained of their simplicity and directness, as being unworthy
of a divine origin. And he adds this positive testimony:
"Her answers, though submitted to the severest scrutiny,
have never proved false or incorrect. On the contrary, the
verification of them has filled the temple with gifts from all
parts of Greece and foreign countries." And again, "The
answer of Pythoness proceeds to the very truth, without any
diversion, circuit, fraud, or ambiguity. It has never yet, in
a single instance, been convicted of falsehood." Would such
statements be made by such a writer, if these oracles were all
the mere guesses of impostors? The fact that they declined
and ultimately failed, is wholly in their favor; for why should
imposture cease as the world became less enlightened and
more superstitious? Neither does the fact that the priests
could sometimes be bribed to give out false oracles prove anything, against such statements as that of Plutarch and the belief during many generations, supported by ever-recurring
experiences, of the greatest men of antiquity. That belief
could only have been formed by demonstrative facts; and
Modern Spiritualism enables us to understand the nature of
those facts.

3. Both the Old and New Testaments are full of Spiritualism, and Spiritualists alone can read the record with an enlightened belief. The hand that wrote upon the wall at Bel-
shazzar's feast, and the three men unhurt in Nebuchadnez-
zar's fiery furnace, are for them actual facts which they need
not explain away. St. Paul's language about "spiritual
gifts," and "trying the spirits," is to them intelligible language, and the "gift of tongues" a simple fact. When Christ
cast out "devils" or evil spirits, he really did so—not merely
startle a madman into momentary quiescence; and the water
changed into wine, as well as the bread and fishes continually
renewed till five thousand men were fed, are credible as extreme manifestations of a power which is still daily at work
among us.

4. The miracles of the saints, when well attested, come
into the same category. Those of St. Bernard, for instance,

were often performed in broad day before thousands of spectators, and were recorded by eye-witnesses. He was himself greatly troubled by them, wondering why this power was bestowed upon him, and fearing lest it should make him less humble. This was not the frame of mind, nor was St. Bernard's the character, of a deluded enthusiast. The Spiritualist need not believe that all this never happened ; or that St. Francis d'Assisi and St. Theresa were not raised into the air, as eye-witnesses declared they were.

5. Witchcraft and witchcraft trials have a new interest for the Spiritualist. He is able to detect hundreds of curious and minute coincidences with phenomena he has himself witnessed ; he is able to separate the *facts* from the absurd *inferences* which people imbued with the frightful superstition of diabolism drew from them, and from which false inferences all the horrors of the witchcraft mania arose. Spiritualism, and Spiritualism alone, gives a rational explanation of witchcraft, and determines how much of it was objective fact, how much subjective illusion.

6. Modern Roman Catholic miracles become intelligible facts. Spirits whose affections and passions are strongly excited in favor of Catholicism, produce those appearances of the Virgin and of saints which they know will tend to increased religious fervor. The appearance itself may be an objective reality ; while it is only an inference that it is the Virgin Mary —an inference which every intelligent Spiritualist would repudiate as in the highest degree improbable.

7. Second-sight, and many of the so-called superstitions of savages, may be realities. It is well known that mediumistic power is more frequent and more energetic in mountainous countries ; and as these are generally inhabited by the less civilized races, the beliefs that are more prevalent there may be due to facts which are more prevalent, and be wrongly imputed to the coincident ignorance. It is known to Spiritualists that the pure dry air of California led to more powerful and more startling manifestations than in any other part of the United States.

8. The recently-discussed question of the efficacy of prayer receives a perfect solution by Spiritualism. Prayer may be often answered, though not directly, by the Deity. Nor does the answer depend wholly on the morality or the religion of the petitioner ; but as men who are both moral and religious, and are firm believers in a divine response to prayer, will pray more frequently, more earnestly and more disinter-

estedly, they will attract toward them a number of spiritual
beings who sympathize with them, and who, when the necessary mediumistic power is present, will be able, as they are
often willing, to answer the prayer. A striking case is that of
George Müller, of Bristol, who has now for forty-four years
depended wholly for his own support, and that of his wonderful charities, on answer to prayer. His "Narrative of
Some of the Lord's Dealings with George Müller" (6th Ed.,
1860), should have been referred to in the late discussion,
since it furnishes a better demonstration that prayer is sometimes really answered, than the hospital experiment proposed
by Sir Henry Thomson could possibly have done. In this
work we have a precise yearly statement of his receipts and
expenditures for many years. He never asked any one or allowed any one to be asked, directly or indirectly, for a pen-
ny. No subscriptions or collections were ever made; yet
from 1830 (when he married without any income whatever)
he has lived, brought up a family, and established institutions
which have steadily increased, till now four thousand orphan
children are educated and in part supported. It has happened hundreds of times that there has been no food in his house
and no money to buy any, or no food or milk or sugar for the
children; yet he never took a loaf or any other article on
credit even for a day; and during the thirty years over which
his narrative extends, neither he nor the hundreds of children dependent upon him for their daily food have ever been
without a regular meal! They have lived, literally, from
hand to mouth; and his one and only resource has been secret prayer. Here is a case which has been going on in the
midst of us for forty years, and is still going on; it has been
published to the world for many years, yet a warm discussion
is carried on by eminent men as to the fact of whether prayer
is or is not answered, and not one of them exhibits the
least knowledge of this most pertinent and illustrative phenomenon! The Spiritualist explains all this as a personal influence. The perfect simplicity, faith, boundless charity and
goodness of George Müller, have enlisted in his cause beings
of a like nature; and his mediumistic powers have enabled
them to work for him by influencing others to send him money, food, clothes, &c., all arriving, as we should say, just in
the nick of time. The numerous letters he received with
these gifts, describing the sudden and uncontrollable impulse
the donors felt to send him a certain definite sum at a certain
fixed time—such being the exact sum he was in want of and

had prayed for—strikingly illustrates the nature of the power at work. All this might be explained away, if it were partial and discontinuous ; but when it continued to supply the daily wants of a life of unexampled charity, *for which no provision in advance was ever made* (for that Müller considered would show want of trust in God), no such explanation can cover the facts.

9. Spiritualism enables us to comprehend and find a place for that long series of disturbances and occult phenomena of various kinds, which occurred previous to what are termed the Modern Spiritual Manifestations. Robert Dale Owen's works give a rather full account of this class of phenomena, which are most accurately recorded and philosophically treated by him. This is not the place to refer to them in detail ; but one of them may be mentioned as showing how large an amount of unexplained mystery there was, even in our own country, before the world heard anything of Modern Spiritualism. In 1841, Major Edward Moor, F. R. S., published a little book called "Bealings Bells," giving an account of mysterious bell-ringing in his house at Great Bealings, Suffolk, and which continued for fifty-three days. Every attempt to discover the cause, by himself, friends, and bell-hangers, were fruitless ; and by no efforts, however violent, could the same clamorous and rapid ringing be produced. He wrote an account to the newspapers, requesting information bearing on the subject, when, in addition to certain wise suggestions—of rats or a monkey as efficient causes—he received fourteen communications, all relating cases of mysterious bell-ringing in different parts of England, many of them lasting much longer than Major Moor's, and all remaining equally unexplained. One lasted eighteen months ; another was in Greenwich Hospital, where neither clerk-of-the-works, bell-hanger, nor men of science could discover the cause. One clergyman wrote of disturbances of a most serious kind continued in his parsonage for *nine years*, and he was able to trace back their existence in the same house for *sixty years*. Another case had lasted *twenty years*, and could be traced back for a *century*. Some of the details of these cases are most instructive. Trick is absolutely the most incredible of all explanations. Spiritualism furnishes the explanation by means of analogous facts occurring every day, and forming part of the great system of phenomena which demonstrates the spiritual theory. Major

Moor's book is very rare ; but a good abstract of it is given in Owen's "Debatable Land," pp. 239–258.

MORAL TEACHINGS OF SPIRITUALISM.

We have now to explain the Theory of Human Nature, which is the outcome of the phenomena taken in their entirety, and is also more or less explicitly taught by the communications which purport to come from spirits. It may be briefly outlined as follows :

1. Man is a duality, consisting of an organized spiritual form, evolved coincidently with and permeating the physical body, and having corresponding organs and developments.

2. Death is the separation of this duality, and effects no change in the spirit, morally or intellectually.

3. Progressive evolution of the intellectual and moral nature is the destiny of individuals ; the knowledge, attainments and experience of earth-life forming the basis of spirit-life.

4. Spirits can communicate through properly-endowed mediums. They are attracted to those they love or sympathize with, and strive to warn, protect, and influence them for good, by mental impression when they cannot effect any more direct communication ; but, as follows from clause (2), their communications will be fallible, and must be judged and tested just as we do those of our fellow-men.

The foregoing outline propositions will suggest a number of questions and difficulties, for the answers to which readers are referred to the works of R. D. Owen, Hudson Tuttle, Professor Hare, and the records of Spiritualism *passim.* Here I must pass on to explain with some amount of detail, how the theory leads to a pure system of morality with sanctions far more powerful and effective than any which either religious systems or philosophy have put forth.

This part of the subject cannot perhaps be better introduced than by referring to some remarks by Professor Huxley in a letter to the Committee of the Dialectical Society. He says, "But supposing the phenomena to be genuine— they do not interest me. If anybody would endow me with the faculty of listening to the chatter of old women and curates at the nearest cathedral town, I should decline the privilege, having better things to do. And if the folk in the spiritual world do not talk more wisely and sensibly than their

friends report them to do, I put them in the same category."
This passage, written with the caustic satire in which the
kind hearted Professor occasionally indulges, can hardly
mean that if it were proved that men really continued to live
after the death of the body, that fact would not interest him,
merely because some of them talked twaddle? Many scientific men deny the spiritual source of the manifestations, on
the ground that real, genuine spirits might reasonably be expected not to indulge in the common-place trivialities which
do undoubtedly form the staple of ordinary spiritual communications. But surely Professor Huxley, as a naturalist and
philosopher, would not admit this to be a reasonable expectation. Does he not hold the doctrine that there can be no effect, mental or physical, without an adequate cause? and
that mental states, faculties, and idiosyncrasies, that are the
result of gradual development and life-long—or even ances-
tral—habit, cannot be suddenly changed by any known or
imaginable cause? And if (as the Professor would probably
admit) a very large majority of those who daily depart this
life are persons addicted to twaddle, persons who spend much
of their time in low or trivial pursuits, persons whose pleasures are sensual rather than intellectual—whence is to come
the transforming power which is suddenly, at the mere
throwing off the physical body, to change these into beings
able to appreciate and delight in high and intellectual pursuits? The thing would be a miracle, the greatest of miracles, and surely Professor Huxley is the last man to contem-
plate innumerable miracles as part of the order of nature ;
and all for what? Merely *to save these people from the necessary consequences of their misspent lives.* For the essential
teaching of Spiritualism is, that we are, all of us, in every act
and thought, helping to build up a "mental fabric," which
will be and constitute ourselves, more completely after the
death of the body than it does now. Just as this fabric is
well or ill built, so will our progress and happiness be aided
or retarded. Just in proportion as we have developed our
higher intellectual and moral nature, or starved it by disuse
and by giving undue prominence to those faculties which se-
cure us mere physical or selfish enjoyment, shall we be well
or ill fitted for the new life we enter on. The noble teaching
of Herbert Spencer, that men are best educated by being left
to suffer the natural consequences of their actions, is the
teaching of Spiritualism as regards the transition to another
phase of life. There will be no imposed rewards or punish-

ments ; but every one will suffer the natural and inevitable
consequences of a well or ill-spent life. The well-spent life
is that in which those faculties which regard our personal
physical well-being are subordinated to those which regard
our social and intellectual well-being, and the well-being of
others ; and that inherent feeling—which is so universal and
so difficult to account for—that these latter constitute our
higher nature, seems also to point to the conclusion that we
are intended for a condition in which the former will be almost wholly unnecessary, and will gradually become rudi-
mentary through disuse, while the latter will receive a corresponding development.

Although, therefore, the twaddle and triviality of so many
of the communications is not one whit more interesting to
sensible Spiritualists than it is to Prof. Huxley, and is never
voluntarily listened to, yet the fact that such poor stuff is
talked (supposing it to come from spirits) is both a fact that
might have been anticipated and a lesson of deep import.
We must remember, too, the character of the séances at
which these commonplace communications are received. A
miscellaneous assemblance of believers of various grades and
tastes, but mostly in search of an evening's amusement, and
of skeptics who look upon all the others as either fools or
knaves, is not likely to attract to itself the more elevated and
refined denizens of the higher spheres, who may well be supposed to feel too much interest in their own new and grand
intellectual existence to waste their energies on either class.
If the fact is proved, that people continue to talk after they
are dead with just as little sense as when alive, but that, being in a state in which sense, both common and uncommon,
is of far greater importance to happiness than it is here
(where fools pass very comfortable lives), they suffer the
penalty of having neglected to cultivate their minds ; and
being so much out of their element in a world where all pleasures are mental, they endeavor to recall old times by gossip-
ing with their former associates whenever they can find the
means—Prof. Huxley will not fail to see its vast importance
as an incentive to that higher education which he is never
weary of advocating. He would assuredly be interested in
anything having a really practical bearing on the present as
well as on the future condition of men ; and it is evident that
even these low and despised phenomena of Spiritualism, "if
true," have this bearing, and, combined with its higher teachings, constitute a great moral agency which may yet regen

erate the world.   For the Spiritualist who, by daily experience, gets absolute knowledge of these facts regarding the
future state—who knows that, just in proportion as he indulges in passion, or selfishness, or the exclusive pursuit of
wealth, and neglects to cultivate the affections and the varied powers of his mind, so does he inevitably prepare for
himself misery in a world in which there are no physical
wants to be provided for, no sensual enjoyments except those
directly associated with the affections and sympathies, no
occupations but those having for their object social and intellectual progress—is impelled toward a pure, a sympathetic,
and an intellectual life by motives far stronger than any
which either religion or philosophy can supply.   He dreads
to give way to passion or to falsehood, to selfishness or to a
life of luxurious physical enjoyment, because he knows that
the natural and inevitable consequences of such habits are
future misery, necessitating a long and arduous struggle in
order to develop anew the faculties, whose exercise long disuse has rendered painful to him.   He will be deterred from
crime by the knowledge that its unforeseen consequences
may cause him ages of remorse ; while the bad passions which
it encourages will be a perpetual torment to himself in a state
of being in which mental emotions cannot be laid aside or for-
gotten amid the fierce struggles and sensual pleasures of a
physical existence.   It must be remembered that these beliefs (unlike those of theology) will have a living efficacy,
because they depend on *facts* occurring again and again in
the family circle, constantly reiterating the same truths as
the result of personal knowledge, and thus bringing home to
the mind, even of the most obtuse, the absolute reality of
that future existence in which our degree of happiness or
misery will be directly dependent on the " mental fabric " we
construct by our daily thoughts and words and actions here.
   Contrast this system of natural and inevitable reward and
retribution, dependent wholly on the proportionate development of our higher mental and moral nature, with the arbi-
trary system of rewards and punishments dependent on
stated acts and beliefs only, as set forth by all dogmatic religions, and who can fail to see that the former is in harmony
with the whole order of Nature—the latter opposed to it.   Yet
it is actually said that Spiritualism is altogether either imposture or delusion, and all its teachings but the product of " expectant attention " and "unconscious cerebration "!   If none
of the long series of demonstrative facts which have been

here sketched out, existed, and its only product were this theory of a future state, that alone would negative such a supposition. And when it is considered that mediums of all grades, whether intelligent or ignorant, and having communications given through them in various direct and indirect ways, are absolutely in accord as to the main features of this theory, what becomes of the gross misstatement that nothing is given through mediums but what they know and believe themselves? The mediums have, almost all, been brought up in some of the usual Orthodox beliefs. How is it, then, that the usual Orthodox notions of heaven are *never* confirmed through them?

In the scores of volumes and pamphlets of spiritual literature I have read, I have found no statement of a spirit describing "winged angels," or "golden harps," or the "throne of God"—to which the humblest orthodox Christian thinks he will be introduced if he goes to heaven at all. There is no more startling and radical opposition to be found between the most diverse religious creeds, than that between the beliefs in which the majority of mediums have been brought up and the doctrines as to a future life that are delivered through them; there is nothing more marvelous in the history of the human mind than the fact that, whether in the back-woods of America or in country towns in England, ignorant men and women having almost all been brought up in the usual sectarian notions of heaven and hell, should, the moment they become seized by the strange power of mediumship, give forth teachings on this subject which are philosophical rather than religious, and which differ wholly from what had been so deeply ingrained into their minds. And this statement is not affected by the fact that communications purport to come from Catholic or Protestant, Mahometan or Hindoo spirits. Because, while such communications maintain special *dogmas* and *doctrines*, yet they confirm the *very facts* which really constitute the spiritual theory, and which in themselves contradict the theory of the sectarian spirits. The Roman Catholic spirit, for instance, does not describe himself as being in either the orthodox purgatory, heaven, or hell; the Evangelical Dissenter who died in the firm conviction that he should certainly "go to Jesus," never describes himself as being with Christ, or as ever having seen him, and so on throughout. Nothing is more common than for religious people at séances to ask questions about God and Christ. In reply they never get more than opinions, or more frequently the statement that they, the spirits, have no more actual knowledge of those subjects than they had while on earth. So that the facts are all harmonious ; and the very circumstance of there being sectarian spirits bears witness in two ways to the truth of the spiritual theory—it shows that the mind, with its ingrained beliefs, is not suddenly changed at death ; and it shows that the communications are not the reflection of the mind of the medium, who is often of the same religion as the communicating spirit, and, because he does not get his own ideas confirmed, is obliged to call in the aid of "Satanic influence" to account for the anomaly.

The doctrine of a future state and of the proper preparation for it as here developed, is to be found in the works of all Spiritualists, in the utterances of all trance-speakers, in the communications through all mediums; and this could be proved, did space permit, by copious quotations. But it varies in form and detail in each ; and just as the historian arrives at the opinions or beliefs of any age or nation, by collating the individual opinions of its best and most popular writers, so do Spiritualists collate the various statements on the subject. They know well that absolute dependence is to be placed on no individual communications. They know that these are received by a complex physical and mental process, both communicator and recipient influencing the result ; and they accept the teachings as to the future state of man only so far as they are repeatedly confirmed in substance (though they may differ in detail) by communications obtained under the most varied circumstances, through mediums of the most different characters and acquirements, at different times and in distant places. Fresh converts are apt to think that, once satisfied the communications come from their deceased friends, they may implicitly trust to them, and apply them universally; as if the vast spiritual world was all molded to one pattern, instead of being, as it almost certainly is, a thousand times more varied than human society on the earth is, or ever has been. The fact that the communications do not agree as to the condition, occupations, pleasures, and capacities of individual spirits, so far from being a difficulty, as has been absurdly supposed, is what ought to have been expected ; while the agreement on the essential features of what we have stated to be the spiritual theory of a future state of existence, is all the more striking, and tends to establish that theory as a fundamental truth.

The assertion so often made, that Spiritualism is the survival or revival of old superstitions, is so utterly unfounded as to be hardly worth notice. A science of human nature which is founded on observed facts ; which appeals only to facts and experiment ; which takes no beliefs on trust ; which inculcates investigation and self-reliance as the first duties of intelligent beings ; which teaches that happiness in a future life can be secured by cultivating and developing to the utmost the higher faculties of our intellectual and moral nature, *and by no other method*—is and must be the natural enemy of all superstition. Spiritualism is an experimental science, and affords the only sure foundation for a true philosophy and a pure religion. It abolishes the terms "supernatural" and "miracle" by an extension of the sphere of law and the realm of nature ; and in doing so it takes up and explains whatever is true in the superstitions and so-called miracles of all ages. It, and it alone, is able to harmonize conflicting creeds ; and it must ultimately lead to concord among mankind in the matter of religion, which has for so many ages been the source of unceasing discord and incalculable evil ; and it will be able to do this because it appeals to evidence instead of faith, and substitutes facts for opinions ; and is thus able to demonstrate the source of much of the teaching that men have so often held to be divine.

It will thus be seen that those who can form no higher conception of the uses of Spiritualism, "even if true," than to detect crime or to name in advance the winner of the Derby, not only prove their own ignorance of the whole subject, but exhibit in a marked degree that partial mental paralysis, the result of a century of materialistic thought, which renders so many men unable seriously to conceive the possibility of a natural continuation of human life after the death of the body. It will be seen also that Spiritualism is no mere "physiological" curiosity, no mere indication of some hitherto unknown "law of nature" ; but that it is a science of vast extent, having the widest, the most important, and the most practical issues, and as such should enlist the sympathies alike of moralists, philosophers and politicians, and of all who have at heart the improvement of society and the permanent elevation of human nature.

In concluding this necessarily imperfect though somewhat lengthy account of a subject about which so little is probably known to most of the readers of the Fortnightly Review, I would earnestly beg them not to satisfy themselves with a

minute criticism of single facts, the evidence for which, in my
brief survey, may be imperfect; but to weigh carefully the
mass of evidence I have adduced, considering its wide range
and various bearings. I would ask them to look rather at the
results produced by the evidence than at the evidence itself
as imperfectly stated by me; to consider the long roll of men
of ability who, commencing the inquiry as skeptics, left it as
believers, and to give these men credit for not having over-
looked, during years of patient inquiry, difficulties which at
once occur to themselves. I would ask them to ponder well
on the fact, that no earnest inquirer has ever come to a conclusion adverse to the reality of the phenomena; and that no
Spiritualist has ever yet given them up as false. I would ask
them, finally, to dwell upon the long series of facts in human
history that Spiritualism explains, and on the noble and sat-
isfying theory of a future life that it unfolds. If they will do
this, I feel confident that the result I have alone aimed at will
be attained; which is, to remove the prejudices and miscon-
ceptions with which the whole subject has been surrounded,
and to incite to unbiased and persevering examination of the
facts. For the cardinal maxim of Spiritualism is, that every
one must find out the truth for himself. It makes no claim
to be received on hearsay evidence; but, on the other hand,
it demands that it be not rejected without patient, honest and
fearless inquiry.

NOW READY.

A BIOGRAPHY

OF

MRS. J. H. CONANT,

The World's Medium of the Nineteenth Century.

A HISTORY OF HER MEDIUMSHIP

From Childhood to the Present Time;

BEING A NARRATIVE OF THE

Personal Experiences, Sharp Trials, and Liberalizing Victories achieved in the cause of Human Reason and Spiritual Knowledge.

Let the heart-stricken read it, and be comforted;
Let the earth-weary peruse it, and be glad;
Let the world's workers explore it, and be encouraged;
Let the doubter scan its incontrovertible testimony, and be confounded;
Let the true man and woman, wherever abiding, recognize in it the
life-line of a *kindred soul.*

COLBY AND RICH,

PUBLISHERS,

NO. 9 MONTGOMERY PLACE,

BOSTON, MASS.

FLASHES OF LIGHT

FROM

THE SPIRIT-LAND,

THROUGH THE MEDIUMSHIP OF

MRS. J. H. CONANT.

COMPILED AND ARRANGED BY

ALLEN PUTNAM,

Author of "Spirit-Works;" "Natty, a Spirit;" "Mesmerism, Spiritualism,
Witchcraft, and Miracle;" Etc., Etc.

This comprehensive volume of more than four hundred pages
will present to the reader a wide range of useful information
upon subjects of the utmost importance.

THE DISEMBODIED MINDS

of many distinguished lights of the past

HERE SPEAK

to the embodied intelligences of to-day, proclaiming their views
as derived from or modified by the FREEDOM FROM ARTIFICIAL
CONSTRAINT, and the ADDED LIGHT OF THE SPIRIT-
WORLD, concerning

THE ORIGIN OF MAN,

the duty devolving upon each individual, and the

DESTINY OF THE RACE.

As an Encyclopædia of Spiritual Information, this work is
without a superior.

Price $1.50.   Postage 22 cents.

COLBY AND RICH, PUBLISHERS,

9 Montgomery Place, Boston.

THE CLERGY

A

SOURCE OF DANGER

TO THE

AMERICAN REPUBLIC.

BY W. F. JAMIESON.

"By being a good Churchman, a person might become a bad citizen."
—*Fox's Speech in the House of Commons, Parl. Hist., Vol. xxix, p.* 1377.

"The king, [George III,] on every occasion, paid a court to the clergy."
"He was, therefore, sure of their support, and they zealously aided him in every attempt to oppress the Colonies."—*Buckle's History of Civilization in England, Vol. i, p.* 343.

"During almost a hundred and fifty years, Europe was afflicted by religious wars, religious massacres, and religious persecutions; not one of which would have arisen, if the great truth had been recognized, that the state has no concern with the opinions of men, and no right to interfere, even in the slightest degree, with the form of worship which they may choose to adopt.—*Buckle's History, p.* 190.

CLOTH	-	-	-	-	-	-	**$1,50**
GILT	-	-	-	-	-	-	**2,00**

POSTAGE 20 CENTS.

ORIGIN AND PROGRESS

OF THE

MOVEMENT FOR THE

RECOGNITION OF THE

CHRISTIAN GOD, JESUS CHRIST

AND THE BIBLE,

IN THE

UNITED STATES CONSTITUTION.

BY W. F. JAMIESON.

PRICE 15 CENTS, POSTAGE 2 CENTS.

A Book for Everybody—Married or Single.

THIS NEW, SEARCHING, TIMELY BOOK IS ENTITLED

"THE GENESIS AND ETHICS OF CONJUGAL LOVE."

By ANDREW JACKSON DAVIS.

WE have the pleasure to announce the recent publication of a fresh, new book, of peculiar interest to all men and women, by this well-known and widely-read author. Treatment of all the delicate and important questions involved in Conjugal Love, is straightforward, unmistakably emphatic, and perfectly explicit and plain in every vital particular. Mr. DAVIS has recently examined the whole field of Marriage, Parentage, Disaffection, and Divorce, and this little volume is the result; which now comes into the world because it is now both wanted and needed by all women and men. The following are some of the

CONTENTS:

Published by the "Progressive Publishing House" of A. J. Davis & Co., No. 24 East Fourth Street, New York City.

Price, in paper covers, 50 cents; in handsome cloth, 75 cents: in full gilt and extra binding, $1.00. Postage free. The Trade supplied on the most liberal terms.

Please make your Post-office Orders payable at "*Station D.*"

Correspondents are respectfully requested to address the Publishers, thus:—

A. J. DAVIS & CO.,
Box 82, Station D,
New York City

SYNOPSIS

OF THE

COMPLETE WORKS OF A. J. DAVIS,

COMPRISING TWENTY-SEVEN UNIFORM VOLUMES, ALL NEATLY
BOUND IN CLOTH.

NO EXTRA CHARGE FOR POSTAGE.

Packages sent C. O. D. to any part of the United States or the World.

Natures' Divine Revelations	$3 50
The Physician. Vol. I. Gt. Harmonia	1 50
The Teacher. " II. "	1 50
The Seer. " III. "	1 50
The Reformer. " IV. "	1 50
The Thinker. " V. "	1 50
Magic Staff—An Autobiography of A. J. Davis	1 75
A Stellar Key to the Summer Land	75
Arabula, or Divine Guest	1 50
Approaching Crisis, or Truth vs. Theology	1 00
Answers to Ever-recurring Questions from the People	1 50
Children's Progressive Lyceum Manual	60
Death and the After-Life	75
History and Philosophy of Evil	75
Harbinger of Health	1 50
Harmonial Man, or Thoughts for the Age	75
Events in the Life of a Seer. (Memoranda.)	1 50
Philosophy of Special Providence	50
Free Thoughts Concerning Religion	75
Penetralia, Containing Harmonial Answers	1 75
Philosophy of Spiritual Intercourse	1 25
The Inner Life, or Spirit Mysteries Explained	1 50
The Temple—on Diseases of Brain and Nerves	1 50
The Fountain, with Jets of New Meanings	1 00
Tale of a Physician, or Seeds and Fruits of Crime	1 00
The Sacred Gospels of Arabula	1 00
Diakka, and their Earthly Victims	50

Price at Regular Retail Rates, $34 10.

☞ The Complete Works of A. J. DAVIS, if ordered to one address, $27 00.

Please make your Post-office Orders payable at "*Station D.*"

☞ *Correspondents are respectfully requested to address us, thus:*—

A. J. DAVIS & CO.,
Box 82, *Station D,*
New York City.

A DEFENCE

OF

MODERN SPIRITUALISM.

BY

ALFRED R. WALLACE, F. R. S.,

AUTHOR OF "THE NATURAL HISTORY OF THE MALAY ARCHIPELAGO,"
"EXPLORATIONS ON THE AMAZON," "THE THEORY
OF NATURAL SELECTION,"
ETC., ETC.

WITH A PREFACE

BY EPES SARGENT.

BOSTON:
COLBY AND RICH,
9 MONTGOMERY PLACE.
1874.